Things Not Seen
and Other Stories

Things Not Seen
and Other Stories

LYNNA WILLIAMS

LITTLE, BROWN AND COMPANY
BOSTON   TORONTO   LONDON

First Edition

The characters and events in this book are fictitious.
Any similarity to real persons, living or dead,
is coincidental and not intended by the author.

Grateful acknowledgment is made to the following publications,
in which some of these pieces were first published:
the *Atlantic*, the *Clinton Street Quarterly*, and *Lear's*.

Library of Congress Cataloging-in-Publication Data

Williams, Lynna.
    Things not seen and other stories / Lynna Williams. — 1st ed.
        p.   cm.
    Contents: Afghanistan — The sisters of desire — Personal
testimony — Sole custody — A morning in the late Cretaceous period
— Last shift at the mine — Rescue the perishing — Legacy —
Things not seen.
    ISBN 0-316-94240-5
    I. Title.
PS3573.I44977T47   1992
813'.54 — dc20   91–47884

10   9   8   7   6   5   4   3   2   1

BP

Published simultaneously in Canada
by Little, Brown & Company (Canada) Limited

Printed in the United States of America

For my parents,
Dorothy and George Williams,
with love and thanks

and for
Richard Bausch:
"First you must teach them;
then you must give them a dollar"

Contents

Acknowledgments

I WOULD LIKE to thank my agent, Miriam Altshuler, for her good humor and support, and my editors, C. Michael Curtis and Karen Dane, for their thoughtful reading of my stories. I would also like to thank Mike Curtis in his role as senior editor of *The Atlantic,* for his encouragement from the very beginning. I owe Pat Stacey more than I can ever repay for her endless editorial and moral support, and Betty Tully, Ron Kurtz, and Ellen Herbert an equal debt for their patient counsel. Richard Bausch and Susan Shreve taught me almost everything I know, both as teachers and as fiction writers, and I thank them, too. My gratitude to Marge Hols and Janice Tucker for always being there, and to Marty and Terrie Williams for the use of the hall. Finally, my love and thanks to the other Bausch groupies: Stacey, Pam, Steve, Oscar, Vera, Dorothy, Bernie, and on and on through the next generation.

Things Not Seen
and Other Stories

Afghanistan

WHEN HOPKINS GOT HOME from covering the Houston Astros' Saturday-afternoon home game against the Reds, he sat in his car for a minute or two, looking at the house where he lived with his wife and daughter. He had been doing this for a week now every time he came home — sitting in the heat and quiet of the car instead of getting out at once, as he had always done before.

He sat there trying not to be impatient, since he had discovered that he could not hurry this; no amount of talking to himself — saying he had to stop it, had to get up, get out of the car, and go inside — did any good until enough time had passed and he was ready.

Now, as he waited for that moment, he thought about the Saturday before, when the routine with the car had started, born of an uneasiness that visited him without warning, just as he was pulling into the drive next to Ellen's car. It was a feeling he couldn't name, but couldn't make go away, either.

He had driven home from the airport after an Astros

away game in San Francisco and, instead of getting out of the car to go in to his family, had continued to sit where he was. Five minutes went by with Hopkins doing nothing but looking at the house where he lived, taking in the second-story shutters that needed painting again; the ungainly sunflowers lining the front porch; the white swing that held a neighbor's sleeping tomcat flanked by two baby dolls. He knew those baby dolls; they were the only offspring of his daughter, Tess, and he had diapered them more than once on long Sunday afternoons in the past.

He had been sure with every new moment that he was about to open the car door and get out — he could see himself doing it, lifting his bag, fumbling with his keys — but still he hadn't moved, not even when Tess appeared at the front door of the house. He saw her, a small figure in shorts and a too-big T-shirt knotted at the waist, waving to him from the doorway fifty feet away. But despite the welcoming pressure in his chest at the sight of his child, he stayed where he was until Tess came to the car and opened the door.

"Daddy, what are you doing?" she had asked. "Mommy's on the phone, but she said to tell you that people shouldn't be sportswriters if losing makes them too sad to come inside the house."

At the sound of that wifely joke in his daughter's mouth, Hopkins had pulled Tess to him, bending down until he could no longer see the house or anything at all but the small, dark head he was kissing hello.

4

"I'm not doing anything, baby," he had said. "Let's go in and see Mom and I'll tell you about California."

Inside the house, Hopkins's sojourn in the car had begun to seem funny; the three of them laughed about it at dinner, Tess announcing that she wanted to go sit behind the wheel to eat her ice cream.

"Ask your father," Ellen had said, and when she and Tess laughed, Hopkins felt the uneasiness leave him; everyone, everything, in this room was familiar, and loved by him. It was not until later that night, in bed, when Ellen moved a hand from his chest and asked, "Billy, what were you doing out there?" that he understood that he truly did not have an answer he could give her, and felt, in the silence, all his troubling unease return.

That had been the beginning; now Hopkins accepted the fact that when he drove home, he would go through the ritual with the car, whatever it was, before he went in. Ellen, and Tess, with her mother's prodding, had stopped referring to it; when he did go into the house, their random gentleness made him aware that they had taken to watching for his car and then waiting for his return to them.

Hopkins got out of the car and let himself into the kitchen through the garage. He knew he was alone in the house — no house where his daughter was could ever be this still — but he called out for Ellen and Tess anyway, before he went to the refrigerator for a beer.

There was a Fritz the Cat Post-it note from Ellen on the door. "Read the note on the TV," it said, and he smiled because his wife never did anything without preamble; the imparting of even basic information went through precise stages.

He reached to pull the note off, no longer smiling — Fritz the Cat communicated trouble, as compared to plain yellow notes or the Snoopy ones she saved for the baby-sitter, and he didn't want trouble, not after a four-hour, 12–0 loss to Cincinnati, and ten minutes alone in the driveway.

He sat at the kitchen table drinking his beer until just enough time had passed to establish that he was going into the living room to watch the news, not just to see what Ellen had to say. Then he got up — a little stiffly because he'd banged his knee on a press-box table at the Astrodome when it looked like the guys might actually score — and hit the door harder than he needed to on the way out of the room.

The TV was against the far wall, but even from the doorway he could make out the leering little Fritz face above Ellen's careful printing. He walked closer, four, five steps, and read out loud, " 'Have gone to Afghanistan. Tess at Scotts' overnight. Food in fridge.' " The Scotts were neighbors, and the food was probably pasta, but Hopkins didn't know what *Afghanistan* meant in his wife's lexicon.

Lexicon was one of Ellen's words; she was in her final year of a master's in linguistics, and she was hell on the patterns and usage of contemporary American speech. "Wussy!" one of Hopkins's buddies from the *Post* sports desk had screamed at an editor at a party the week before, and the other wives had tightened their mouths and for the rest of the evening their husbands had worked overtime showing *they* knew that sex-linked pejoratives were no different from race-linked pejoratives.

Not Hopkins, though, because Ellen was over in the corner splitting a Saint Pauli Girl with the screamer, interviewing him about where he had first heard the word, and its layers of meaning for him. "Scout camp in sixth grade," Hopkins heard her say. "That's fascinating. Now tell me what *beaver* means to you."

So *Afghanistan* was one of Ellen's code words, Hopkins thought, but what was the code? He considered it while drinking the last of the beer, but nothing came to him. It was cool in the living room — Ellen must have turned the air-conditioning on high before she and Tess left — but Hopkins felt moisture collecting on the back of his neck. The sweat, the smallest beading above the collar of his knit shirt, seemed to have some connection to his spine, pulling it upward; feeling it, he slouched, a deep and resolute slouch that, he was proud to see in the mirror opposite, was absolutely not the stance of a man who was worried.

He felt the unease he had tried to confine to the car return — it straddled his shoulders now, riding him the way Tess did in the home-team bleachers — but he told himself he had nothing to worry about. He knew Ellen would never leave Tess with the Scotts if something was really wrong; they were Republicans, and his wife was polite to them only out of compassion for their seven-year-old, who was named Brandee Chantal.

"Why didn't they just call her Clerical Help?" Ellen always asked after Brandee came over to play with Tess. "With those names, that's exactly what she's going to do with her life."

Every time Ellen said that, it occurred to Hopkins that he didn't want Tess growing up to contract tuberculosis and marry a wastrel, which was what her name had suggested to him when Ellen had first picked it out. But he knew the name spoke different images to his wife, and that was the whole point: words, all words, spoke volumes to Ellen. Hopkins had a hundred examples crowding his mind of her attention to their selection and meaning, so *Afghanistan* meant — what did *Afghanistan* mean?

He reached for the phone on the sofa table and looked at the numbers on the pad next to it until he found the Scotts'. When Mrs. Scott answered — her name was Carol Ann — he asked to speak to Tess.

"Hi, baby," he said when she came on. "I just wanted to know how you were."

"I'm fine, Daddy, but we're playing My Little Ponies, and I need to go."

"I just need a minute. Mom left me a note, but I'm not sure where she is. Did she tell you where she was going?"

8

There was silence while Tess turned away from the phone; Hopkins could hear her shouting at Brandee, "I want the red nail polish for my pony; you promised!"

"Tess? Are you there, baby?"

"I'm sorry, Daddy, Brandee was hogging the red."

"Did your mother —" Hopkins began again, but Tess was talking.

"She said she was going to — I don't know, I can't remember."

Hopkins thought of the word games that Ellen had played with Tess at bedtime for years, and feeling a little as though he were Peter Falk shaking down a seven-year-old witness to a crime, he said, "Try, Tess, please."

"Apple," she said obediently.

"Appalachia?" from Hopkins.

"Announcement?" from Tess, who went on, "Accent. Aunt." She was gathering speed, Hopkins could tell, and he knew from experience that she would go on trying out *A* words until she left for college, unless he stopped her. He knew where this was leading, anyway, and he brought the word out now, softly.

"Afghanistan? Tess, was it Afghanistan?"

"Da-ad." This word was two syllables, what Ellen called Tessanese, and it meant, "Why did you ask me if you already knew?" She started to say his name again but then stopped, giggling.

"What's funny, baby?"

"Mommy. Brandee's mom just always says she's going to Safeway."

9

"Go play ponies, baby. I'll see you tomorrow."

She was gone then, and Hopkins replaced the receiver. The question he had not asked — "Did Mom say she'd pick you up tomorrow?" — seemed to be rolling, end over end, in a path between his stomach and his throat, and feeling slightly sick, he went into the bedroom and lay down on the bed.

The digital clock flipped to 7:23 as he looked around the room; the closet door was open, and he could see the neat arrangement of Ellen's clothes and shoes. "Looks like everything's there," he said aloud, mocking himself a little because he was scared now. He could admit that, he thought. When he left for the ball game, at noon, Ellen was at home on the couch in the den, analyzing folk poetry for sound, and when he got home, at six-thirty, she was gone; Clint Eastwood would be scared by now, and Phil Donahue — Phil Donahue would be in intensive care at Memorial Hospital.

Hopkins lay still, trying to coax some enjoyment out of an image of Phil Donahue tearing around Telephone Road on a Saturday night looking in the parking lots of seedy bars for Marlo Thomas. When the picture failed to make him smile — made him, in fact, a little sad for Phil's predicament — he switched to looking hard at the bedroom door, willing Ellen to come walking through it, smiling, carrying her books or a Foley's shopping bag or two. That was no good at all, and he got up to go back into the kitchen, feeling anyplace would be better than the bedroom, where his wife was everywhere but nowhere to be seen.

In the kitchen, he stooped to root around in the refrigerator for the dinner Ellen's note had said would be there, and emerged with a casserole dish with stuffed pasta shells. While his dinner was heating, he leaned against the sink, thinking about where he could go to look for her. The truth was, he didn't know where to go; he knew Ellen's usual routes — back and forth between the university, the library, Safeway, Tess's school, the bank, the laundry, Saint Stephen's Episcopal, the park — but he didn't think any of those everyday places would be her Afghanistan.

Still thinking about it, he put dinner on the table, doing a little Texas two-step across the tile to the sink after he put his hand on the hot dish without stopping to get the pot holder. He ate quickly, writing notes to himself in the notebook he'd used to cover the game. He drew a line through the last sentence of an interview with the outfielder Finley and wrote AFGHANISTAN in capital letters. Then, in the way he'd seen Ellen do when she was trying to think of connections for new words she'd heard, he wrote *Country. Mountainous. Rugged. Afghan Rebels. Invasion. Russians,* and, after some deliberation, *Khurds.* He wasn't sure about that last, so he crossed it out and wrote *Freedom Fighters.*

Then he read the list out loud. He didn't like the way *freedom* sounded in his mouth with Ellen God knows where, so he concentrated on *mountainous,* which had a nice roll to it. He turned his head at a sudden image of Ellen on the edge of a green hillside, her face alive with interest as she quizzed an Afghan rebel about the origins of the term . . . The image faded because he didn't know any of the words his wife would be using in her new life in Afghanistan.

He poked hard at a pasta shell, a part of him hearing Ellen tell him he was too literal. His wife was skittish about heights and personally offended by dirt; she wasn't likely to be gracing an actual Afghan hillside unless it had an actual Sheraton Inn, and even then, she'd take her own towels. But he didn't feel like laughing. There was nothing metaphorical about Ellen's absence; it was after 9:00 P.M. now, and wherever she was, she wasn't with him.

He pulled the phone on the kitchen counter over to the table. When the *Post* reference desk answered, he said, "Merrilee, hi, this is Hopkins; do something for me, will you?"

The reference staff hated sports; he could hear her breathing, thinking hard, before she said, "Okay, but don't you yell at me. It's not my fault newspapers have deadlines."

"Of course it's not. Could you just pull the jacket on Afghanistan and read me whatever story's on top? Whatever's the last one we ran?"

She was gone for a long time, and when she came

back she said, "It wasn't in the sports files. I had to look in news."

Hopkins paused — he was imagining the headline: AFGHANS PLAYING HURT; VOW COMEBACK — before he said, "I appreciate that, Merrilee. What does the top story say?"

She began reading, in a school-recitation style that reminded Hopkins of Tess's when she brought home a new pop-up book from the library. AFGHAN LEFT FEELS BETRAYED BY RUSSIANS was the headline on the *New York Times* wire story; although Merrilee went on reading, Hopkins stopped listening.

When Merrilee was done, he thanked her and hung up. He had no logical reason for the certainty, but he was sure, and had been since he heard the word in Merrilee's little-girl voice. He knew what *Afghanistan* meant to Ellen. It meant betrayal.

Hopkins got up from the kitchen table fast, banging his right knee all over again, and half limped into the hall, headed for the front door. He didn't know where he was going to look for Ellen, exactly, but he did know he couldn't stay in their house, inhabited as it now was not by him and Ellen but only by himself and the fact of his betrayal of her.

In the hall, he dropped, and then kicked, his keys. When he bent to retrieve them and straightened up, he saw his face again in the living-room mirror. Staring up at himself in recognition, he realized there was another meaning that Ellen could have attached to the word and the act of betrayal. He understood then that she might be referring not to *his* infidelity, over and done with for weeks, but to her own, happening now.

∽∾

When Tess was little, not even walking yet, Ellen's mother had called from Fort Worth to say that her sister, the aunt Ellen loved best, had been diagnosed with liver cancer and wasn't expected to live through the month. Ellen didn't want to take Tess to Fort Worth, but she didn't want to let her aunt die without saying a proper good-bye, either. Hopkins was working all the hours God made, the *Post* sports desk at night, grad school at Rice during the day, but he told Ellen to go, that he'd take some vacation and stay with Tess while she was gone.

The first day without Ellen was fine. Tess kept looking around for her mother, as though she'd simply misplaced her somewhere and would surely come across her anytime now, but she wasn't frantic about it, just curious. She and Hopkins spent the day together trying out things that neither of them did, for whatever reason, when Ellen was home.

Hopkins read the sports page out loud to his daughter, lingering over the women's pro golf scores. "Nancy Lopez wins another tournament, Tessie," he said in her baby ear, clapping her hands together while she stared at him. "And she's going to give all the money to her daddy! Good girl, Nancy, good girl." Later they watched the all-sports channel on cable, Hopkins holding Tess in his lap and doing his own play-by-play. At a replay of a French Open match, the camera panned the gallery, and there, right in the front row, was Nancy Lopez. "Tess, look, there's Nancy," Hopkins said, and it seemed to him for a moment that her baby eyes, gray like her mother's, solemnly followed his finger.

Tess confined her new activities to the kitchen; she threw most of her breakfast on the floor and, finding that to her liking, most of her lunch. At dinner that night, Hopkins stood in front of her high chair, watching her warily, like a pitcher with a wild kid at the plate. "Baby batter, baby batter, pretty little baby batter," he chanted, and then, "Whoa, close one there, baby," as Tess eyed him with perfect good humor and a fistful of strained peas.

When dinner was over — all over him, mostly — Hopkins left Tess bouncing up and down in her high chair and went into the bedroom to get both of them a change of clothes. He was still there, his head halfway through a Rice Owls sweatshirt, when he heard a crash. For a moment there was no sound at all from the baby, and then, just as Hopkins started the run to the kitchen, there was a cry, and then a scream.

When he got to the kitchen, he saw Tess amid the ruin of the high chair, which apparently had tipped to one side and then fallen. She was on her side, caught half in, half out of the chair; what he could see of her face was contorted, readying for another scream.

He scooped her up — it was then that he saw the blood streaking her left cheek — and, calling her name over and over, ran with her to the car, where he strapped her in her seat for the three-block drive to the hospital ER. They made it in two minutes; Tess never stopped screaming, but to Hopkins, listening, it seemed a wonderful sound because he had some idea that the noise might stop, that Tess might fall silent and die.

At the emergency room, a circle of hands took the baby from him and someone else led him to the lounge, where he was told to sit until a doctor came for him. As soon as he was still, without Tess to anchor him to what needed to be done, Hopkins began to shake. He sat in the chair, feeling tremors run the length of his body; after each one came the aftershocks, the guilt that made it impossible to breathe or think or do anything but hold tight to the arms of the chair, seeing the face of his daughter as she lay on the dirty kitchen tile.

He had left his child in a high chair unattended, and now she was hurt and afraid and with strangers. Hopkins could not move with the enormity of the responsibility pressing in on him; he simply sat, feeling it, until a young doctor in hospital greens came in and told him that Tess was fine — a cut on her forehead, bruised and frightened, but perfectly sound.

A minute later his child was in the room, brought to him by a nurse who called her "precious pie" and said she was cute enough to eat. Tess was silent with Hopkins, and wary — he could see that she was trembling, too — but once in his arms she turned and buried her face in his chest.

Back at home, Hopkins was unable to leave Tess in her crib and go to his bed to sleep. After a while he carried her to the bed and arranged every pillow in the house around her so that she simply could not fall. But that wasn't enough, either, and at about midnight he put a quilt on the floor and lay there with her next to him, certain at last that she was safe.

The next morning he woke to find Tess stuffing her fist in his mouth, rocking to some baby wake-up call all her own. As he pulled her onto his chest to kiss her, the guilt was there.

It was there when he fed her and changed her and bathed her, when he called Ellen to tell her what he had done, when he dropped off to sleep a second night with Tess beside him on the floor. When he picked her up the next morning to start all over again, he did it with the guilt still on him, as real a presence as Tess herself, who was at that moment gripping his arm with her tiny fingers. He thought then that the guilt would always be with him, would always be a part of how he was with his daughter, a part of who he was.

But then Ellen had come home and Tess was fine and days, weeks, went by, until slowly the feeling went away. He remembered it, with a kind of recognition that made him reach out a hand for something to hold, when he woke in a bed not his own, beside a woman who was not Ellen.

☙

In nine years of marriage, Hopkins had been unfaithful to his wife in his heart maybe two times, in his head probably a half dozen more, and with all of himself exactly once, the month before, with a magazine reporter in town from Chicago.

He had risen from her bed at about two in the morning, tasting panic as strong as the beer and Chinese food they'd shared, and begun gathering his things to go home, as though the speed with which he got there would make things right. He said his good-byes and made his apologies; he listened as the woman he had slept with talked; he waited while both of them said everything over again. All the time he was dressing, putting on his shoes and socks, his shirt and pants, until he stood in the doorway and said again that he had been terribly wrong, that there was no excuse he could make, and that he was sorry.

He drove home slowly — he was supposed to be putting the sports page to bed after an Astros night game — and let himself in the back door. Ellen was asleep when he got into bed, but she turned toward him and mumbled something he thought was his name. He lay down next to her, carefully, as though any moves not planned in advance might jar the truth out of him. He fell asleep with his fingertips touching his mouth, the same gesture

Tess used to signal for absolute quiet when she was It in hide-and-seek.

⤫

Three weeks after that night, the routine with the car started — three weeks in which Hopkins's guilt grew, and with it his need to confess — and he understood that he would have to tell Ellen what he had done. It was clear she already knew something was wrong. He could tell by her determination to give him time to come to her; her shakes of the head at Tess when they thought he wasn't looking; the precision of the words she used when they did talk, as though any looseness of speech from her might add to his sorrow, whatever it was.

He watched her reading to Tess when he worked at home and needed quiet; telling stories from the English department to make him laugh; serving peach ice cream on apple pie because he liked it that way; and he began to feel the guilt as a physical presence: in any room he entered, there were Ellen and Tess, and there was the guilt he carried with him.

He had chosen the night before last to tell Ellen, a night when Tess was playing at the Scotts'. When he and Ellen were through with dinner, he told her he'd do the dishes later and asked her to please come sit with him on the couch. She sat down willingly, balancing a glass of wine on her knee, and said, "So are you going to talk to me now? What is it? You've gambled our adjoining plots at Roseland away at the dog track? You want to send Tess to military school? What? Billy, tell me."

She reached for his hand, but he pulled away from her and stood up. "Ellen, don't." He started to go on, but the rest of it — the words he had practiced over and over — was lost to him as he looked at her and realized for the first time what he was about to do. To sidestep the guilt somehow, to go into a long slide that would bring him home safely, that was what he wanted, but that had to do with being able to breathe again; it had nothing to do with loving Ellen.

She was still looking at him when he took the hand she had offered him a moment before and lowered himself onto the couch next to her. "I love you, Ellen," he said, and that, at least, was true. "I never want anything to hurt you." Hearing those words, Hopkins knew he was not going to tell his wife any other truths that night, and he closed his eyes against the feeling that, finally, he had done something right.

When he opened them, he saw Ellen staring at him with the steady, unwavering stare of a stranger. She did not speak, but instead got up and walked toward the bedroom. Hopkins followed her, praying that he was wrong but knowing he was not. He had not needed to say the words out loud about what he had done, he thought. Ellen had heard him anyway.

In the car, Hopkins sat for a minute, leaning forward so that his forehead was touching the steering wheel, before he backed out of the driveway. He automatically headed the car in the direction of the newspaper, but before he'd gone five blocks, he pulled over. He had to decide where he was going, but the temptation to just sit there — to give in to the feeling that the solution to all this was nowhere he could drive to in a Honda — was growing stronger. To combat it, he turned off the air-conditioning and rolled the window down.

It was so hot the air seemed solid, as though it had welcomed his car into the darkness and then closed in again around it. The night seemed to have absorbed both light and sound; there was just one porch light burning the length of the street, and the only sounds he could hear came from that same house, where a woman's voice was calling her child to come in now. The words were ordinary; he had used them many times himself to bring Tess in from outdoors. But something about the woman's voice sounded wrong to him — too high, too plaintive — and he quickly rolled up the window.

He had to look for Ellen. He knew he wasn't going to find her; he knew, too, that the real business between them would be conducted tomorrow or later tonight, whenever she came home. But he kept driving. He needed to do something. The alternative was to go back to the house and wait for whatever was going to happen, and that was no alternative at all. In the house, Ellen's absence was palpable; it made the familiar rooms of their home seem like places he was entering for the first time. In the car, at least, the question of her whereabouts seemed not smaller, exactly, but more closely contained.

At the stoplight at Brazewood, he turned down Telephone Road, a strip of bars and restaurants south of downtown. He couldn't remember the last time he'd been down here, but he knew it would have been with a group from the paper, not with Ellen. She wasn't interested in drunks or noise or fried food, which were three of Telephone Road's attractions. The other cornerstone of this part of town's reputation — that men and women came here to be unfaithful, in whatever ways they could — Hopkins tried not to think about at all. He could not look at any of these places and imagine his wife inside, but part of him thought this might be as close to Afghanistan, to heat and dust and betrayal, as Houston had to offer.

He drove down the strip once, slowly, and then turned around and went back the other way. He peered into every parking lot, exactly as he had imagined Phil Donahue doing earlier, but even if Ellen's car was here somewhere, it was too dark to see it.

On his second run out of town, he stopped at Blackie's, the city's biggest bar and dance hall, and stood for a minute in the night air. He watched as four couples came out the front door together and then separated to look for their car, until one of the women called out, "It's over here, Danny! I see it!" The whole crowd converged on the car she was pointing to and, when it turned out to be not even close to the right one, laughed and fanned out again.

"Sweet Jesus, Leitha, that's a Volvo!" one of the men called back over his shoulder, and they all laughed. "How're you tonight, buddy?" the same man said to Hopkins when he passed, and Hopkins nodded his head. He thought suddenly that he might just turn and ask to go with them — they seemed so happy, so sure that what they were looking for was out here somewhere — but he went on walking toward the bar entrance.

Inside Blackie's, he stood at the front until he could see in the darkness. The dance floor, empty now, was to his left, and the bar itself was straight ahead, with chairs arranged in a wide circle around it and more tables on both sides. Hopkins sat down at the bar and asked for a beer; he drank it slowly, all of it, before he looked around the room.

Ellen wasn't here; it took him only a few seconds to scan the room and make sure of it. He had known she wouldn't be, but he couldn't tell whether it was disappointment or relief that made him turn quickly back to the bar. As he did, a woman sat down in the seat next to his and said hello.

She was probably twenty-five, about six or seven years younger than Ellen, Hopkins thought, pretty in a way that suggested determination more than anything else. She wore no wedding band, just a high school ring with a red stone. As she waited for her drink, Hopkins noticed her rub her finger where a gold band would have been.

He turned away, as though he had seen too much, and was getting up to go when he noticed how many other women there were sitting by themselves in the bar. When he had looked around before, he had seen only that none of them was Ellen, but now he counted four women alone before he stopped, not wanting to go any higher. He did not know if these women were married or single, happy or sad, missing or accounted for, but they seemed to fill up the room — to be, all at once, everywhere that he looked and all that he could see.

"Are you all right?" he heard the woman next to him say, and he made himself focus on her.

"I'm okay, thank you," he said, but the concern on her face didn't lessen and he didn't know for a moment if he had said the words out loud. He thanked her again then and got up to leave. For the first time since he had seen himself in the mirror at home, the knowledge that Ellen might be sitting somewhere like this, across town, across Texas, across an ocean, for all he knew, seemed real to him. He wanted her — he wanted her with him in some safe and familiar place. He pushed open the bar door and went out into the darkness, heading home.

At the house, Hopkins opened the garage door, hoping that Ellen's car would be inside. It wasn't, and he drove in and then let himself into the house through the door to the kitchen. He didn't linger in the car; the man who had been doing that all week had no idea of how to save his marriage from himself, and Hopkins did know.

He went through the house, turning on every light for company, and then back into the living room to wait for Ellen. He sat on the couch and ran over what he would say when his wife came home.

He imagined the scene, seeing himself first, sitting on this same blue paisley couch that he and Ellen had picked out the March Tess had chicken pox. In his vision he was leaning forward just as he was now, earnestly talking to an Ellen whose face was half turned toward the door. She was rising to go, reaching for a suitcase by her chair, but in his imagination Hopkins did not falter. He went on talking, quietly, confidently, about the exact meaning of the word *love*.

The Sisters of Desire

BEFORE THE SADNESS took her, Chris was an English graduate student, deconstructing Andrew Marvell with her brightness and her almost-Ph.D., but by the day one late, wet spring when Tom Duffin came to stand beside her in the clinic waiting room, she had assembled a much longer list of everything she had once been but no longer was: she was not a doctoral candidate anymore, but she was also not Brian's wife, nor a mother-to-be, nor a good daughter. She had been ambitious, and vaguely religious, and a Democrat, and sentimental about animals, and vain about her hair; she was none of those things now. She had been deconstructed — she had broken down — and now she was this Chris Goodwin, not herself again because she would never be that exactly, but not sad, either, not in the way she had been. She was a dark-haired woman, almost pretty, dutifully reading the *Star-Telegram* want ads before her two-o'clock appointment with Maria, and when the tall man in the khaki pants said her name, she looked up and smiled, not at him at all, not this first time. She was

27

smiling because in a dozen small ways she was happy to be here, sitting on a scarred couch in a county mental-health clinic, her feet tucked under her, a half-inch of banner-red sock showing between her jeans and running shoes.

When she looked up, she thought to herself that she knew who this was, or at least what he was. He was a county caseworker, not a therapist; his office was two up from Maria's, and when Chris walked down the hall and his door was open, she could hear him explaining disability payments, or coaxing a landlord to return a deposit. If he looked up and saw her, he always smiled; he was doing it now.

"Chris Goodwin?" he said, and when she nodded, "And I'm Tom, Tom Duffin; can we talk for a minute?"

When she said yes, he sat down beside her on the couch. He didn't crowd her. He kept his distance, and she looked at him, interested. Some people — not Maria — pushed, shoved in too close, too fast, but this man apparently was not that kind.

"Maria tells me you're looking for part-time work while you decide things, and I was wondering if you'd be interested in some baby-sitting?"

When Chris hesitated, wondering what else Maria might have told him, Maria who knew everything, he went on talking. She recognized it as technique: he was going slow, giving her time to react. He was good at it, too, Chris thought; anyone passing by — anyone who had never been crazy — would have thought he was her friend.

"My stepdaughter, Rachel, is eleven; she's probably old enough to stay by herself some of the time, but her mother and I are gone a lot, and we like for someone to be with her. We have a sitter now for after school, and she was going to stay with Rachel this summer. But she told us last week she's moving to Peoria to be a lounge singer. She swears the place is called the Top-Hat Club; do you think that's possible?"

Chris looked at him, but he appeared to think it was a serious question. "They have to call it something," she said. "Would you go to a lounge called the Fumes-from-the-Tire-Factory Club?"

Tom laughed, and Chris liked that; she had to be careful around Maria, who was from El Salvador and regarded Lucille Ball as the last truly funny American.

"So Stacey's Peoria-bound, and Rachel's miserable. They had all sorts of things planned for the summer, and she's convinced her life is over."

Chris had lost odd memories to the depression; first grade was intact, but four summers at camp and the first year of her marriage were mostly gone. Sometimes, to compensate, she made up childhood stories, straight-faced, with a literature major's ease. "The same thing happened to me when I was Rachel's age," she said, and stopped, startled, because this was a true story. "My next-door neighbor Pam baby-sat for me until she went to college. I wouldn't admit for months how much I liked the woman my parents got next. She taught me to use a camera. All Pam ever did was braid my hair."

"If you can remember what it was like to be an eleven-year-old, Rachel will love you. She's always accusing her mother of forgetting, and I'm not an authority on little girls. Having a daughter's new for me, and anyway, Rachel and I are both convinced she's smarter than I am. It's terrifying sometimes, let me tell you."

Chris smiled. "What night would you want me to come?"

"This Saturday; Sherry and I have a hospital dinner to go to. If you and Rachel hit it off, we can see if you're interested in staying with her days during the summer. Her school's out in another two weeks, so we have to find someone soon. What do you think? Do you want to give Saturday night a try?"

Chris had been making small decisions for months. She picked an apartment when she came out of the hospital; she planned her meals around the cents-off coupons in the paper; she juggled which bills to pay which months; she set up small, careful routines: calling her mother in Killeen on Wednesday nights when the rates changed; rereading Shakespeare's history plays, in order, but leaving the tragedies strictly alone; going to church every Sunday, not to pray but to sing the hymns.

She had made no big decisions at all — she was an acolyte of small, deliberate steps, of going slowly — but

30

she looked at Tom Duffin and said, "Saturday's fine, and I'm interested in the summer job, too."

He smiled at her again. Chris was unimpressed by professional good cheer, but she decided that Tom was smiling at her specifically. He was seeing her as she was now, and he was smiling.

There was more: he handed her the address and told her some things about Rachel's allergies, and Chris matched him smile for smile, nodding, laughing once, all the while feeling the folded square of paper smooth against her palm. When Tom left her, she went down the clinic hallway to Maria's office and announced that she must be a grown-up again: she had a job. She was about to add that it was only a night of baby-sitting, and maybe a summer job, but Maria didn't give her a chance to say it. She stood, hugged Chris hard, and then used up half of the fifty-minute session on an elaborate parable, loosely adapted, as far as Chris could make out, from *The Little Engine That Could*. Maria's stock of inspirational stories came mostly from children's programming on PBS.

When she left the clinic, Chris walked back to her apartment a different way, cutting across Tenth Street to go past an elementary school. It was midafternoon, and there were children on the playground playing kickball. Chris stood by the fence watching them, trying to pick out girls Rachel's age, wondering if Rachel would be a tomboy, wondering if Rachel would like her, and then she thought about Tom Duffin — how he had taken his time talking to her, and the polite way he'd asked her if she was busy Saturday night, when he must have known from Maria that she hadn't been busy for months.

Chris had gone into the hospital in October, and on days when the sadness had permitted, she'd sometimes made lists of all the people she'd stopped loving, starting with her mother and going all the way to David. She left the hospital not loving anyone, and she began another list, this one of people she could bring herself to like. Maria was first. Chris watched the children playing and decided that if she did some rearranging, Tom Duffin could be second.

Chris stayed at the Duffins' for the first time that Saturday night in May. At the end of the evening, when Rachel had finally been talked into going to bed, Chris sat on the window seat in the living room and waited for Tom and Sherry to come home and offer her the summer job watching Rachel. Chris was careful about wanting things, but she wanted the job.

Rachel had taken charge from the beginning. When Tom and Sherry left, she led Chris into the kitchen, where the two of them fixed hamburgers for dinner, Rachel talking faster and faster, about her school, her mother and Tom, her father's death when she was "little," her ballet lessons, her plans to be a doctor like her mother. After Rachel's bath, when Chris said good night upstairs, Rachel jumped up to hug her, still talking, standing on her bed so that she was taller than Chris, opening her arms to pull Chris toward her. "I'm glad you're feeling better," Rachel whispered, and she kissed Chris on the cheek.

Chris was not ashamed, or defensive; she didn't ask herself how much Rachel knew. She answered, "Thank you, sweetie; sleep tight," and walked to the door to turn out the light. She walked softly, almost warily, because she knew that she was taking something with her from Rachel's bedside, something precious, some new feeling to which she could not put an exact name but which clearly was a fixed and distant galaxy away from sadness.

She wasn't just charmed by Rachel, though, Chris thought as she sat in the window, listening now to Mozart, watching the darkness take the cottonwood trees that outlined the backyard, drinking lemon tea from a china cup. She loved the idea of herself here, in this storybook house, with this storybook family.

When Tom and Sherry came home at midnight, Chris was waiting for them with a pot of tea. Tom carried it to the sunroom, where the three of them sat and talked about Rachel. They were laughing over a story of Tom's — about his first appearance at a slumber party — when Rachel appeared at the door in her pajamas, pushing her baby-fine black hair out of her eyes with her fingers.

"Rachel, what are you doing up?" Sherry said. "Is something wrong?"

Rachel walked to the porch swing and made a place for herself next to her mother. "I want Chris to stay with me this summer," she said. "I didn't go to sleep because you have to ask her before she goes home. I don't want anybody else; please."

"We're talking about it now," Sherry said. "Chris has to decide what she wants, too."

Chris sat on the floor drinking her tea, her back against a wicker plant stand that held a giant Boston fern. She put her cup down before she got up, walking quickly to join the family in the greater light across the room.

❧

Rachel dragged her mother's Indian blanket off the guest bed and spread it on the grass behind the house. She and Chris stretched out on it, taking turns calling out names for what they saw as they watched the only cloud in the July sky drifting into new shapes above them.

"Rabbit," Rachel said.

"Cowboy hat," Chris said, resting on one elbow and tilting her head back to get a better look.

"Mormon elder." The last was Rachel's, and the game stopped because they were both laughing. They'd checked out all the Sherlock Holmes stories their last time at the library, and Rachel was reliving *A Study in Scarlet*. She saw nineteenth-century Mormons everywhere.

"Mormon death lizard," Rachel said.

"That's it, kiddo," Chris said. "Back to Laura Ingalls Wilder for you."

"Little House on the Mormon Prairie," Rachel said under her breath, and Chris groaned and cupped her hands over her ears. Rachel was quiet then, and after a few minutes, Chris thought she must have fallen asleep. She sat up to look at her. Rachel's animation defined her; when Chris closed her eyes and thought *Rachel,* she saw moving pictures, mouth and arms, legs and eyebrows, even hair, never quite at rest.

Studying her, Chris thought, as she always did, how different Rachel was when she was still. Her knowing expression, equal parts intelligence and bravado, disappeared, making her look not innocent so much as simply reduced somehow. Chris didn't like seeing her that way — exposed as a child — because she knew her next thought would be about something happening to Rachel. To stop it, she reached across and put her hand on Rachel's shoulder to wake her.

"It's too hot out here, Rach," she said. "Let's go inside." Rachel didn't answer, didn't move at all, and Chris went up on her knees, ready to do CPR or run for the phone to call 911. "Rachel. Rachel, sweetheart, answer me."

She stood then, praying that this was her imagination, but still turning, ready to run to the house and the phone. In that instant, she heard a sound behind her and twisted back to see Rachel sitting up, alive and laughing.

"Mormon paramedics," Rachel said, and when Chris didn't laugh, she put a hand to her mouth, trying to look contrite. "I'm sorry," she said. "It's just so easy to scare you."

"It's a lousy thing to do," Chris said, lowering herself back down on the blanket. "How would you like it if I did that to you?"

Rachel didn't answer, only sat with her head down, so that her face was half veiled by hair. "I love Tom," she said. "You love him, too, don't you, Chris? We both love him."

Rachel was talking fast; the words ran together so that it took Chris a moment to separate them out, to realize that Rachel was not just talking about friendship and affection. Rachel knew. Chris concentrated on staying perfectly still, feeling the heat gather on the back of her neck and legs like an accusation.

Rachel put her hand out, and Chris realized she was being offered comfort. Without thinking, she put her hand around Rachel's smaller one and got up. The two of them walked to the sunroom, slowly, holding hands. It was only when they were settled into the swing that Chris understood that she'd walked past the moment when she could have made a joke of this. She and Rachel had a million jokes between them, but Chris hadn't laughed; she had let the words stand — "You love him, too, don't you, Chris?" — and now it was too late.

Chris thought about Rachel, who was hers to protect from eight to five, Mondays through Fridays, and knew she had to try. She turned in the swing until she was facing Rachel. "Sweetie, listen to me. I know you're confused about how you feel about Tom, and that's okay; he's a wonderful man, and you're still getting used to having a stepfather. You can talk to your mom and Tom about how you feel, and they'll help you with it. But you're wrong about me, Rachel. Tom's been very kind to me, but he loves your mother."

Rachel didn't answer, didn't give any sign that she had heard, but in the next moment she was off the swing, running through the door to the house. Chris called after her, "Rachel, wait," and was getting up to go after her when the door banged open again and Rachel was back, standing there with a legal pad and a pencil.

Chris had a sudden image of herself confessing everything while Rachel — dressed like Maria, in Salvadorean ready-to-wear — took everything down with a No. 2 pencil. The absurdity of it made her able to ask, "Rachel, what is going on?" in the same way she had asked it the day before, when a pizza deliveryman had shown up at the door at lunchtime.

"We'll make a club," Rachel said. "A club for us because we love Tom. Come on, Chris, we'll have secret meetings and a name and everything. I think I should be president, though, since it was my idea."

Chris grabbed for Rachel's arm — she had to make her listen — but Rachel took a step backward. She was standing on one foot, the other drawn up behind her, and Chris saw clearly that she was a child. Rachel was a child and this was a game, and Chris laughed. She had imagined disaster where there was none: Rachel had a crush on Tom, anyone could see that, but she was too young to understand that Chris's feelings were different. The relief was so great that Chris stood and pulled Rachel to her. "It's a deal," she said. "You can be president."

❧

The name was first. They took the legal pad to the cool of the kitchen and sat across from each other at the table, Rachel grandly taking notes as she talked. "It has to be something just the two of us will understand, and scary-sounding, you know, like the names of the secret clubs in Sherlock Holmes. And *sisters*. It has to have *sisters* in it, because there's two of us and we do things together like sisters would."

There was a sticky patch on her left cheek from a lunchtime cherry Popsicle, and Chris loved her. It was an uncomplicated feeling, and she loved that, too — that she could have a feeling that simply was, and did not require explanations.

"*Sisters,* okay, *sisters,*" Rachel said. "What's a word for wanting something, Chris?"

"*Covet. Crave. Wish. Prize.* Oh, Rachel, I don't know. *Desire?*"

As she said it, Chris shifted in her seat because *desire* was a real word, not a play one, and all her unease returned. This was dangerous. But it was too late; Rachel

was writing *The Sisters of Desire* on the legal pad, big, so
that the words filled a whole page in her blocky print.

"It's perfect. Chris, don't you think it's perfect?"

Chris didn't answer. *The Sisters of Desire,* she thought,
amazed that those four small words in combination
could make her, instantly, as ashamed as she had ever
been. She was about to suggest some other name when
she saw, unbidden, an image of all the things she wanted
most but could not have: Tom, and this house of gifts
and grace he came home to every night; the last year of
her life to do over again, to put right from the first, small
sadness; and this child. She wanted Rachel, who sat looking at her now, to be her child, hers and Tom's.

None of it was possible; Chris understood that. But
as she looked at Rachel, who knew a girl's longing but
almost nothing of disappointment, she decided to give
her what she could.

"It's a wonderful name, Rachel."

❧

The end-of-the-day routine had been established during
Chris's first week in the Duffin house; it was in the re-
peating of it, day after day, that she acknowledged to
herself — and to no one else, not even Maria — that she
loved Tom. She knew it was hopeless; she knew it was
a cliché; she knew, most of all, that she wasn't going to
get what she wanted. But still she waited for him to
come home every night. He was usually in the house by
five-thirty, an hour or so before Sherry came home from
the hospital, and he and Chris and Rachel always sat

down together in the quiet of the sunroom for a few minutes before Chris left. She tried not to, but sometimes she imagined she was welcoming Tom home to a house they shared together: offering him iced tea made with mint from the garden, exchanging stories about their days, talking easily about the child who sat facing them on the swing.

Tonight Chris didn't try to stop herself. As Rachel poured the tea and handed Tom cheese and crackers on a silver tray she'd unearthed from the breakfront, Chris watched the two of them with new eyes, as if they really did belong to her.

Tom was thin, showing too much bone in the khakis and short-sleeved shirts he wore to work most days. He was rueful about his face, which was ordinary, and careful of his hair, which was as fine and black as Rachel's. He listened carefully now as Rachel launched into a complicated story about a visit to the Y swimming pool, interrupting to ask questions and registering shock and amazement at all the proper points.

Rachel was caught up both in her own performance and in Tom's reactions. When he gave her a pretend shake at the story's punch line, she shot a triumphant look at Chris, as if some point had been made, and pirouetted away into the kitchen, leaving Chris and Tom alone.

"Amazing how long wedding presents last," Tom said, looking down at the silver tray and then at Chris.

They both smiled at the unspoken "Longer than some marriages." Tom had been married once before, to an environmental lawyer who had left him for a Greenpeace activist. Chris knew the story because he and Sherry exchanged rueful jokes about it sometimes. Chris's breakup with Brian had begun while she was in the hospital. She knew Tom was treating her as a friend, making fun of his own failures with no thought of hers, but still she had to concentrate to keep smiling.

When Rachel came back into the room, Chris was glad to look away. She felt the familiar tension — of having once been sick, of being well now — but tonight she felt a tension, too, in the weight of Rachel in the room, the child who had said out loud that Chris loved Tom. It seemed to Chris, uneasy in the swing, that there was too much knowledge in the room, and too many secrets. She watched Tom and Rachel, their dark heads bent over the movie listings in the *Star-Telegram,* and saw again how separate she was, and would always be, from them, through history and circumstance, through all the things she felt but could not say.

She was thinking about that when Sherry came home, and the Duffins made a family of three while Chris sat, a little apart, holding tight to a glass of tea that was mostly water now.

Sherry was only a little taller than Rachel, but no one ever believed that unless the two of them were standing side by side. She had a doctor's impatience, not wasting motion or words, and both Rachel and Tom did what she said, with Tom making a joke of it sometimes until she stopped issuing orders and relaxed.

He was doing it now, reacting in mock horror to the list of things she wanted done before dinner, and she smiled suddenly and reached up to kiss him. When she did that, she was lovely in a way that recalled the child at her feet, and Chris felt an ache start deep in her chest. Something about the way in which Sherry's hand lingered on Tom's face, the casualness of it, seemed, all at once, too much for her to bear. Chris stood up and said her good-nights, determined to get out of the house before the longing showed in her face and everyone knew what Rachel knew.

Rachel walked her to the front door — Tom and Sherry, discussing dinner, echoed good-nights but did not look up — and motioned for her to bend down. "The Sisters of Desire," she whispered, and Chris hugged her once, hard, before she went down the front steps.

On the street, she walked until she was out of sight of the house. She stopped before she got to the bus stop and sat down on a bench in front of an apartment building. There were tears in her eyes, but she ignored them. She had cried too much to be impressed by her own tears; she sat still, concentrating on her anger at not being able to control this, not being able to stop wanting the life in the Duffin house to be her own.

"The Sisters of Desire," she said aloud, and she let the tears come.

∞

The other patients in the hospital psych ward had talked about the times and places they "went crazy," as though crazy were somewhere they had driven themselves on a summer afternoon.

Chris's place in the group sessions held Monday and Wednesday mornings had been by the far wall, her back to a bank of windows. She sat cross-legged on a pillow brought from her room and counted the wallpaper roses opposite her, listening to the stories other people told. Sometimes she pretended she was back in a graduate seminar on Russian literature, and at those moments the tears that oppressed her were not tears at all, but snowflakes dotting a Moscow street.

Once or twice a week, Chris's turn to speak had come. She spoke in simple sentences — another small thing she could control — and held off crying until she was done. She tended to remember her trouble only in terms of effects, only in terms of things.

She always came back to the doll.

She had walked home from a morning class to the house she and Brian shared with another grad-school couple and their baby. She had wanted to move when their roommates' daughter, Maggie, was born — Chris had miscarried late in her own pregnancy, two months before — but Brian said they couldn't afford their own

43

apartment, and to please try to make do until summer, when he'd be working full-time. Chris tried, and when she walked into a room where the baby was, her housemates tried to remember to be kind.

No one else was at home when Chris put her books on the table and went upstairs to lie down. On the landing, she stopped to listen and realized the sound she was hearing was no sound; the noise in the hall bathroom had stopped.

The toilet had been running for weeks. She had called the landlord, but the serviceman he'd promised had never come, and she'd taken to asking Brian to fix it every morning before he left for school. He always said he'd try, but the noise never stopped. It didn't seem to bother anyone but Chris, but it kept her awake nights, and she was already sleeping too much during the days.

She went into the bathroom, relishing the quiet, and looked down at the toilet. She'd taken the lid off several times herself, trying to figure out what was wrong, but the inner workings of things baffled her, and she always gave up. Now she bent over to lift the lid again, curious to see if she could tell what had been done.

A baby doll lay faceup in the tank, wedged between two levers so that the top one rested at a higher angle than it had before. That lever was across the doll's stomach, and the doll's blond head was just above water, its blue eyes half open. Chris had seen the doll before; it was a gift for Maggie, who was too young still to know what it was.

Chris lifted the doll by the arm to free it from the levers. At her touch, it made a mewling noise that seemed to her, suddenly, the saddest sound possible in the world. She wrapped the doll in a towel and sat on the bathroom floor holding it, listening to the running noise from the toilet. She was still there when Brian came home from school. He made her get up and walked her into the bedroom, but he couldn't make her let go of the doll.

He told her patiently, over and over, that he was sorry, he hadn't stopped to think, he'd put the doll in the tank to make the noise stop until the plumber came — it was the right size, he kept saying — but Chris only looked at him and held the baby doll tighter.

She could hear Brian talking, saying her name into the telephone and then to her — "Chris, oh, Jesus, Chris!" — but there was nothing familiar about him, nothing she could hold on to. What was familiar was what she held in her arms.

When the ambulance came, Chris let herself be taken downstairs, walking ahead of Brian and the paramedics. She spoke only once, when the younger medic reached for the doll so he could take Chris's pulse at the wrist. "She's mine," she said. "Please don't take her. She's been wet and I'm afraid she'll get sick."

"Why don't you let me take her temperature to make sure she's all right?" the man answered, kneeling beside Chris to put a thermometer to the doll's lips. "She's fine, ma'am, and she's sure a pretty baby. Do you think I could hold her? My daughter's about this age."

Chris shook her head no — he was a nice young man, but babies caught things too easily to be passed around — and he said that was all right. Babies were precious, he said, and Chris nodded because here was someone who understood.

By August the Sisters of Desire were meeting every morning, and the club had become, in a gradual way that Chris couldn't trace to one day or one event, the heart of her time with Rachel. At 8:00 A.M., when Chris got to the Duffin house, Rachel would greet her at the door and pull her back to the sunroom, where a breakfast of cinnamon toast and instant coffee would already be arranged on the silver tray. They'd eat, Rachel shoving down the food in her eagerness to begin. Chris would eat more slowly, and Rachel would watch every bite, sometimes grabbing the last piece of toast before Chris could reach for it. "Chris," Rachel would say, "that's enough!" and, clearing her throat, she'd begin the official club report for the day.

Rachel never talked about Chris's loving Tom anymore; Chris's role in the proceedings had narrowed to being an audience for Rachel's talking about Tom. Chris was glad enough of the turn things had taken. She couldn't see any harm in Rachel's adoration for Tom, which seemed natural in a child who had lost her father when she was still too young to remember him. Rachel hadn't talked about her father since the night she and Chris met, but some of the stories she told over and over were about the years she and her mother had spent alone, moving around from medical school to training hospitals in Houston and Fort Worth. She was matter-of-fact about it all, but Chris saw what Rachel had seen: Tom was Prince Charming, the man Rachel had conjured into being with her daydreams and page after page of pencil drawings in her pink, five-year diary.

This morning Rachel talked about how she and Tom had gone to see *Raiders* the night before; about what Tom had said to her about their taking a painting class together at the arts center, just the two of them; and about how Sherry had told her she was proud she was adjusting so well to having a stepfather.

"My mom says she can't believe how well Tom and I get along," Rachel said.

"It is hard to believe anyone gets along with you." Chris waited as Rachel took two steps toward her and collapsed into her lap, laughing.

"I love you, Chris. It's just been the best summer."

Chris didn't answer for a minute; she was thinking about the two weeks left to her in the Duffin house. It had come to her slowly, with a certainty she did not question, whom she loved best in this house. When she dreamed of the Duffin house now, it was always the same: Tom was in the picture, close by but out of frame;

no matter what room they were in, Chris was in the center, where she belonged, as Rachel's mother.

❧

For Chris's last week on the job, Rachel got her mother's permission for a special day when Chris would sleep over while Tom and Sherry were out late at a benefit dinner-dance. Rachel was so excited she agreed to skip the Sisters of Desire meeting that morning. "We'll do it later," she told Chris. "I've got a surprise for you, anyway."

Chris narrowed her eyes at the word *surprise,* but Rachel wouldn't tell her what it was. "You'll see," she kept saying. "It's the greatest thing."

Chris was going back to TCU in the fall — only one theory course, no decision yet about reentering the doctoral program — and she and Rachel started the day by walking to the campus together to celebrate. They stopped for Cokes in the Hop malt shop, and when Rachel asked what coeds ate, Chris solemnly went over the menu, pointing out foods she had eaten as an undergraduate and then as a grad student.

"Don't order the meat loaf," a boy sitting alone at the table next to theirs leaned over to say to Rachel. "It doesn't just *look* the same as when your mom went here; it *is* the same."

Rachel giggled, but she didn't explain that Chris wasn't her mother. She just swung around in her chair until she was facing the boy and began an easy conversation, reporting back to Chris that he was a freshman biology major from Tulsa.

"Well, well," Chris said when the boy had gone, and Rachel nodded, in perfect understanding. It was a woman's nod, full of appreciation and a little irony, and Chris saw the adult that Rachel would become in this animated child eating the last french fry and tapping her foot in time to "Unchained Melody" on the jukebox.

From that moment, the day was as good as any Chris could remember; after TCU, she and Rachel went to a movie house on the West Side and watched Bette Davis in *All About Eve,* and from there they went to Neiman-Marcus and modeled hats in the three-way mirrors.

When the two of them got home that night, Tom and Sherry had already gone out, and as Chris dropped exhausted into a chair, she felt again what she had failed to identify that first night upstairs, the night Rachel kissed her. It was joy, she knew that now. That it wouldn't last didn't seem as important as simply feeling all of it, for as long as she could.

"So what's my surprise?" she said to Rachel, who had pulled herself up and was going into the kitchen to start what she called the "speciality of the house," pasta salad and garlic bread.

"After dinner," Rachel said. "You'll love it, I promise."

That was all she would say until they'd eaten and watched a movie on TV and the two of them got up to get ready for bed. They climbed the narrow stairs together to Rachel's private kingdom, a room created for her from the old attic. When Chris turned around from putting on her nightgown, Rachel was waiting, sitting on her bed with the Sisters of Desire notebook by her side.

"This is my surprise?" Chris asked. "We're having night meetings now, like the Klan?"

"What's the Klan?" Rachel said, and when Chris started to answer, she interrupted, "No, don't tell me now. It's time to start."

As Chris watched, smiling a little, Rachel got up and turned the overhead light off, so that the room was lit only by her ballerina lamp.

"There," she said, turning around and coming back to sit on the bed by Chris. "The last meeting of the Sisters of Desire is called to order. First, the club would like to thank Ms. Goodwin for all her service over the last weeks. You've been a fine and valued member, and we won't forget you."

"Thank you, Madam President," Chris said, as solemnly as Rachel. "It's been a pleasure to serve."

"And now," Rachel said, reaching under the bed for a package and handing it to Chris, "open this."

It was a leather volume of Sherlock Holmes, with a dedication in Rachel's best handwriting, all the letters leaning backward: *To Chris, with love, Rachel,* and then underneath, in parentheses, *The Sisters of Desire, 1985.*

Chris pulled Rachel to her, kissing the top of her head. "It's absolutely perfect," she said through tears. "For a horrible kid, you give great surprises."

"That's how much you know," Rachel said. "That's a present. We haven't gotten to the surprise."

With that, she got up from the bed and walked to the far wall, where she knelt for a moment before turning and sitting on the floor, motioning for Chris to join her.

Chris went to her. "Give me a hint here, kid," she said. "What am I looking at?"

Rachel pointed down and with her hand pulled a smallish piece of the flooring nearest the wall completely up, exposing a space about four inches long and two inches wide.

"The surprise is you're putting in a new floor without telling your parents? Rachel, what on earth do you think you're doing?"

"Look," Rachel said impatiently, and Chris bent over the hole, squinting into the darkness below.

"Look at what? Come on, Rachel, this isn't funny."

"It's their bedroom, don't you get it? Tom and my mom's bedroom. We can see everything that happens when they get home."

Chris stood and pulled Rachel along with her, until they were on their feet and facing each other. "Rachel, no. We can't do that. It's spying, and it's wrong."

Rachel's hands were on her hips, and she looked first at Chris and then down at the floor and her surprise. "We're not going to hurt anyone," she said. "We'll just listen to them talk for a while and see if they say anything about us. It's the club's last meeting, Chris. Please."

"No. What your mom and Tom do is private, Rachel.

Just please put the floor back and let's talk about something else. Come on, now."

Rachel did as she was told, silently. When she was done, she went over to her bed and lay down on top of the covers, her face to the wall.

"Rachel, don't be like that. I'm sorry your surprise didn't work out, but I love my book, and today was great. Please don't spoil it."

"*You* spoiled it," Rachel said to the wall.

Chris waited a minute before she got into the other bed; Rachel didn't say anything more. Chris fell asleep listening for her, still holding Sherlock Holmes.

∾

Chris woke to the tiniest of sounds in the night, instantly suppressed, and sat up, trying to see into the darkness of Rachel's room. "Rachel," she whispered, "are you there? Rachel?"

There was no answer, and Chris got up, feeling her way toward Rachel's bed. She was only halfway there when she heard the same sound again and turned, realizing that Rachel was somewhere behind her. She went back the other way, edging along the wall, until she found the ballerina lamp and turned it on. When she did, she saw Rachel sitting by the wall, her head down, her face buried in her knees.

Chris ran to her, too angry to speak, but when she reached Rachel and knelt down, she forgot everything else. Rachel was crying, without sound, and she let Chris pull her into her lap and put her arms around her. As

Chris did that, she looked down at the floor and heard what Rachel had heard, the sounds of Tom and Sherry making love.

"Oh, sweetheart, oh, Rachel," Chris said, rocking Rachel back and forth in her arms. Rachel didn't speak; she was crying harder now, her breath coming in hard little gasps.

Looking over Rachel, down at the hole, Chris thought she saw the moment when the sounds from above registered on Tom and Sherry. The two figures, lit by a seam of light from behind their bathroom door, let go of each other — Sherry rolling away to the far side of the bed — and then sat up to stare in the direction of the sound. "Rachel?" Chris heard Sherry say. "Rachel?"

In another moment there was the sound of footsteps from the bedroom below, and then on the stairs. Chris stayed where she was, holding Rachel, knowing that everything was finished for her in this house but concentrating only on the child she was holding for the last time, the child whose tears were soaking the front of her nightgown and her skin underneath. Baby's tears, Chris thought, and she held Rachel tighter.

But when Sherry ran into the room, followed by Tom, Chris gave their child to them without a protest and went unnoticed to the far side of the room, where she sat on Rachel's bed. Once she thought Tom turned to look for her, but he was only reaching for the glass of water Rachel kept on her desk.

"Mommy," Rachel said over and over. "Mommy."

"I'm here, sweetie," Sherry said, just as Chris had done. "Hush now, baby, I'm here."

After a long time, when Rachel was quieter, Chris got up, her clothes bunched in her hand, and walked to the door. "Chris," Tom said after her, but she did not stop. In the hallway she turned back, once, to fix in her mind the picture the three of them made, father, mother, and child, and then went forward, down the stairs. She moved quickly, her only regret that on all those hot, bright days she had sat with Rachel on the sunroom swing, she had never once thought to instruct her, slowly, step-by-step, in all she had learned, not only about desire and despair but about surviving the certain intersection of the two, just when everything was happiest and sadness seemed a lifetime away.

Personal Testimony

THE LAST NIGHT of church camp, 1963, and I am sitting in the front row of the junior mixed-voice choir looking out on the crowd in the big sanctuary tent. The tent glows, green and white and unexpected, in the Oklahoma night; our choir director, Dr. Bledsoe, has schooled us in the sudden crescendos needed to compete with the sounds cars make when their drivers cut the corner after a night at the bars on Highway 10 and see the tent rising out of the plain for the first time. The tent is new to Faith Camp this year, a gift to God and the Southern Baptist Convention from the owner of a small circus who repented, and then retired, in nearby Oklahoma City. It is widely rumored among the campers that Mr. Talliferro came to Jesus late in life, after having what my mother would call Life Experiences. Now he walks through camp with the unfailing good humor of a man who, after years of begging hard-scrabble farmers to forsake their fields for an afternoon of elephants and acrobats, has finally found a real draw: his weekly talks to the senior boys on "Sin and the

Circus" incorporate a standing-room-only question-and-answer period, and no one ever leaves early.

Although I know I will never be allowed in the tent to hear one of Mr. Talliferro's talks — I will not be twelve forever, but I will always be a girl — I am encouraged by his late arrival into our Fellowship of Believers. I will take my time, too, I think: first I will go to high school, to college, to bed with a boy, to New York. (I think of those last two items as one since, as little as I know about sex, I do know it is not something I will ever be able to do in the same time zone as my mother.) Then when I'm fifty-two or so and have had, like Mr. Talliferro, sufficient Life Experiences, I'll move back to west Texas and repent.

Normally, thoughts of that touching — and distant — scene of repentance are how I entertain myself during evening worship service. But tonight I am unable to work up any enthusiasm for the vision of myself sweeping into my hometown to Be Forgiven. For once my thoughts are entirely on the worship service ahead.

My place in the choir is in the middle of six other girls from my father's church in Fort Worth; we are dressed alike in white lace-trimmed wash-and-wear blouses from J. C. Penney and modest navy pedal pushers that stop exactly three inches from our white socks and tennis shoes. We are also alike in having mothers who regard travel irons as an essential accessory to Christian Young Womanhood; our matching outfits are, therefore, neatly ironed.

56

At least their outfits are. I have been coming to this camp in the southwestern equivalent of the Saraha Desert for six years now, and I know that when it is a hundred degrees at sunset, cotton wilts. When I used my iron I did the front of my blouse and the pants, so I wouldn't stand out, and trusted that anyone standing behind me would think I was wrinkled from the heat.

Last summer, or the summer before, when I was still riding the line that separates good girls from bad, this small deception would have bothered me. This year I am twelve and a criminal. Moral niceties are lost on me. I am singing "Just as I Am" with the choir and I have three hundred dollars in my white Bible, folded and taped over John 3:16.

Since camp started three weeks ago, I have operated a business in the arts and crafts cabin in the break between afternoon Bible study and segregated (boys only/ girls only) swimming. The senior boys, the same ones who are learning critical new information from Mr. Talliferro every week, are paying me to write the personal testimonies we are all expected to give at evening worship service.

We do not dwell on personal motivation in my family. When my brother, David, and I sin, it is the deed my parents talk about, not mitigating circumstances, and the deed they punish. This careful emphasis on what we do, never on why we do it, has affected David and me differently. He is a good boy, endlessly kind and cheerful and responsible, but his heroes are not the men my father followed into the ministry. David gives God and our father every outward sign of respect, but he worships Clarence Darrow and the law. At fifteen, he has been my defense lawyer for years.

While David wants to defend the world, I am only interested in defending myself. I know exactly why I have started the testimony business: I am doing it to get back at my father. I am doing it because I am adopted.

Even though I assure my customers with every sale that we will not get caught, I never write a testimony without imagining public exposure of my wrongdoing. The scene is so familiar to me that I do not have to close my eyes to see it: the summons to the camp director's office and the door closing behind me; the shocked faces of other campers when the news leaks out; the Baptist Academy girls who comb their hair and go in pairs, bravely, to offer my brother comfort; the automatic rotation of my name to the top of everyone's prayer list. I spend hours imagining the small details of my shame, always leading to the moment when my father, called from Fort Worth to take me home, arrives at camp.

That will be my moment. I have done something so terrible that even my father will not be able to keep it a secret. I am doing this because of my father's secrets.

෨෬

We had only been home from church for a few minutes; it was my ninth birthday, and when my father called me to come downstairs to his study, I was still wearing the dress my mother had made for the occasion, pink dotted swiss with a white satin sash. David came out of his room to ask me what I had done this time — he likes to be prepared for court — but I told him not to worry, that I was wholly innocent of any crime in the weeks just before my birthday. At the bottom of the stairs I saw my mother walk out of the study and knew I was right not to be concerned: in matters of discipline my mother and father never work alone. At the door it came to me: my father was going to tell me I was old enough to go with him now and then to churches in other cities. David had been to Atlanta and New Orleans and a dozen little Texas towns; my turn had finally come.

My father was standing by the window. At the sound of my patent-leather shoes sliding across the hardwood floor, he turned and motioned for me to sit on the sofa. He cleared his throat; it was a sermon noise I had heard hundreds of times, and I knew that he had prepared whatever he was going to say.

All thoughts of ordering room-service hamburgers in an Atlanta hotel left me — prepared remarks meant we were dealing with life or death or salvation — and I wished for my mother and David. My father said, "This is hard for your mother; she wanted to be here, but it upsets her so, we thought I should talk to you alone." We had left any territory I knew, and I sat up straight to listen, as though I were still in church.

My father, still talking, took my hands in his; after a moment I recognized the weight of his Baylor ring against my skin as something from my old life, the one in which I had woken up that morning a nine-year-old, dressed for church in my birthday dress, and come home.

My father talked and talked and talked; I stopped listening. I had grown up singing about the power of blood. I required no lengthy explanation of what it meant to be adopted. It meant I was not my father's child. It meant I was a secret, even from myself.

In the three years since that day in my father's study, I have realized, of course, that I am not my mother's child, either. But I have never believed that she was responsible for the lie about my birth. It is my father I blame. I am not allowed to talk about my adoption outside my family ("It would only hurt your mother," my father says. "Do you want to hurt your mother?"). Although I am universally regarded by the women of our church as a Child Who Wouldn't Know a Rule If One Reached Up and Bit Her in the Face, I do keep this one. My stomach hurts when I even think about telling anyone, but it hurts, too, when I think about having another mother and father somewhere. When the pain is enough to make me cry, I try to talk to my parents about it, but my mother's face changes even before I can get the first question out, and my father always follows her out of the room. "You're our child," he says when he returns. "We love you, and you're ours."

I let him hug me, but I am thinking that I have never heard my father tell a lie before. I am not his child. Not

60

in the way David is, not in the way I believed I was. Later I remember that lie and decide that all the secrecy is for my father's benefit, that he is ashamed to tell the world that I am not his child because he is ashamed of me. I think about the Ford my father bought in Dallas three years ago; it has never run right, but he will not take it back. I think about that when I am sitting in my bunk with a flashlight, writing testimonies to the power of God's love.

My father is one reason I am handcrafting Christian testimonies while my bunkmates are making place mats from Popsicle sticks. There is another reason: I'm good at it.

Nothing else has changed. I remain Right Fielder for Life in the daily softball games. The sincerity of my belief in Jesus is perennially suspect among the most pious, and most popular, campers. And I am still the only girl who, in six years of regular attendance, has failed to advance even one step in Girls' Auxiliary. (Other, younger girls have made it all the way to Queen Regent with Scepter, while I remain a perpetual Lady-in-Waiting.) Until this year, only the strength of my family connections has kept me from sinking as low in the camp hierarchy as Cassie Mosley, who lisps and wears colorful native costumes that her missionary parents send from Africa.

I arrived at camp this summer as I do every year, resigned and braced to endure but buoyed by a fantasy life that I believe is unrivaled among twelve-year-old Baptist girls. But on our second night here, the promise of fish sticks and carrot salad hanging in the air, Bobby Dunn came and stood behind me in the cafeteria line.

Bobby Dunn, blond, ambitious, and in love with Jesus, is Faith Camp's standard for male perfection. He is David's friend, but he has spoken to me only once, on the baseball field last year, when he suggested that my unhealthy fear of the ball was really a failure to trust God's plan for my life. Since that day I have taken some comfort in noticing that Bobby Dunn follows the Scripture reading by moving his finger along the text.

Feeling him next to me, I took a breath, wondering if Bobby, like other campers in other years, had decided to attempt to bring me to a better understanding of what it means to serve Jesus. But he was already talking, congratulating me on my testimony at evening worship service the night before. (I speak publicly at camp twice every summer, the exact number required by some mysterious formula that allows me to be left alone the rest of the time.)

"You put it just right," he said. "Now me, I know what I want to say, but it comes out all wrong. I've prayed about it, and it seems to be God wants me to do better."

He looked at me hard, and I realized it was my turn to say something. Nothing came to me, though, since I agreed with him completely. He does suffer from what my saintly brother, after one particularly gruesome revival meeting, took to calling Jesus Jaw, a malady that makes it impossible for the devoted to say what they mean and sit down. Finally I said what my mother says to the ladies seeking comfort in the Dorcas Bible class: "Can I help?" Before I could take it back, Bobby Dunn had me by the hand and was pulling me across the cafeteria to a table in the far corner.

The idea of my writing testimonies for other campers — a sort of ghostwriting service for Jesus, as Bobby Dunn saw it — was Bobby's, but before we got up from the table, I had refined it and made it mine. The next afternoon in the arts and crafts cabin I made my first sale: five dollars for a two-minute testimony detailing how God gave Michael Bush the strength to stop swearing. Bobby was shocked when the money changed hands — I could see him thinking, Temple. Moneylenders. Jee-sus! — but Michael Bush is the son of an Austin car dealer, and he quoted his earthly father's scripture: "You get what you pay for."

Michael, who made me a professional writer with money he earned polishing used station wagons, is a sweet, slow-talking athlete from Bishop Military School. He'd been dateless for months and was convinced it was because the Baptist Academy girls had heard that he has a tendency to take the Lord's name in vain on difficult fourth downs. After his testimony that night, Michael left the tent with Patsy Lewis, but he waved good night to me.

For an underground business, I have as much word-of-mouth trade from the senior boys as I can handle. I estimate that my volume is second only to that of the snack stand that sells snow cones. Like the snow-cone stand, I have high prices and limited hours of operation. I arrive at the arts and crafts cabin every day at 2:00 P.M., carrying half-finished pot holders from the day before, and senior boys drift in and out for the next twenty minutes. I talk to each customer, take notes, and deliver the finished product by 5:00 P.M. the next day. My prices start at five dollars for words only and go up to twenty dollars for words and concept.

Bobby Dunn has appointed himself my sales force; he recruits customers who he thinks need my services and gives each one a talk about the need for secrecy. Bobby will not accept money from me as payment — he reminds me hourly that he is doing this for Jesus — but he is glad to be thanked in testimonies.

By the beginning of the second week of camp, our director, Reverend Stewart, and the camp counselors were openly rejoicing about the power of the Spirit at work, as reflected in the moving personal testimonies being given night after night. Bobby Dunn has been testifying every other night and smiling at me at breakfast every morning. Patsy Lewis has taught me how to set my hair on big rollers, and I let it dry while I sit up writing testimonies. I have a perfect pageboy, a white Bible bulging with five-dollar bills, and I am popular. There are times when I forget my father.

❧

On this last night of camp I am still at large. But although I have not been caught, I have decided I am not cut out to be a small business. There is the question of good help, for one thing. Bobby Dunn is no good for detail work — clearly, the less he knows about how my mind works, the better — and so I have turned to Missy Tucker. Missy loves Jesus and her father and disapproves of everything about me. I love her because she truly believes I can be saved and, until that happens, is willing to get into almost any trouble I can think of, provided I do not try to stop her from quoting the appropriate Scripture. Even so, she resisted being drawn into the testimony business for more than a week, giving in only after I sank low enough to introduce her to Bobby Dunn and point out that she would be able to apply her cut to the high cost of braces.

The truth is, the business needs Missy. I am no better a disciple of the Palmer Handwriting Method than I am of Christ or of my mother's standards of behavior. No one can read my writing. Missy has won the penmanship medal at E. M. Morrow Elementary School so many times there is talk that it will be retired when we go off to junior high in the fall. When she's done writing, my testimonies look like poems.

The value of Missy's cursive writing skills, however, is offset by the ways in which she manifests herself as a True Believer. I can tolerate the Scripture quoting, but her fears are something else. I am afraid of snakes and of not being asked to pledge my mother's sorority at

Baylor, both standard fears in Cabin A. Missy is terrified of Eastern religions.

Her father, a religion professor at a small Baptist college, has two passions: world religions and big-game hunting. In our neighborhood, where not rotating the tires on the family Ford on a schedule is considered eccentric, Dr. Tucker wears a safari jacket to class and greets everyone the same way: "Hi, wallaby." Missy is not allowed to be afraid of the dead animals in her father's den, but a pronounced sensitivity to Oriental mysticism is thought to be acceptable in a young girl.

Unless I watch her, Missy cannot be trusted to resist inserting a paragraph into every testimony in which the speaker thanks the Lord Jesus for not having allowed him or her to be born a Buddhist. I tell Missy repeatedly that if every member of the camp baseball team suddenly begins to compare and contrast Zen and the tenets of Southern Baptist fundamentalism in his three-minute testimony, someone — even in this trusting place — is going to start to wonder.

She says she sees my point but keeps arguing for more "spiritual" content in the testimonies, a position in which she is enthusiastically supported by Bobby Dunn. Missy and Bobby have fallen in love; Bobby asked her to wear his friendship ring two nights ago, using his own words. What is art to me is faith — and now love — to Missy, and we are not as close as we were three weeks ago.

I am a success, but a lonely one, since there is no one

I can talk to about either my success or my feelings. My brother, David, who normally can be counted on to protect me from myself and others, has only vague, Christian concern for me these days. He has fallen in love with Denise Meeker, universally regarded as the most spiritually developed girl in camp history, and he is talking about following my father into the ministry. I believe that when Denise goes home to Corpus Christi, David will remember law school, but in the meantime he is no comfort to me.

Now, from my place in the front row of the choir, I know that I will not have to worry about a going-out-of-business sale. What I have secretly wished for all summer is about to happen. I am going to get caught.

Ten minutes ago, during Reverend Stewart's introduction of visitors from the pulpit, I looked out at the crowd in the tent and saw my father walking down the center aisle. As I watched, he stopped every few rows to shake hands and say hello, as casual and full of good humor as if this were his church on a Sunday morning. He is a handsome man, and when he stopped at the pew near the front where David is sitting, I was struck by how much my father and brother look alike, their dark heads together as they smiled and hugged. I think of David as belonging to me, not to my father, but there was an unmistakable sameness in their movements that caught me by surprise, and my eyes filled with tears.

Suddenly David pointed toward the choir, at me, and my father nodded his head and continued walking toward the front of the tent. I knew he had seen me, and I concentrated on looking straight ahead as he mounted the stairs to the stage and took a seat to the left of the altar. Reverend Stewart introduced him as the special guest preacher for the last night of camp, and for an instant I let myself believe that was the only reason he had come. He would preach and we would go home together tomorrow. Everything would be all right.

I hear a choked-off sound from my left and know without turning to look that it is Missy, about to cry. She has seen my father, too, and I touch her hand to remind her that no one will believe she was at fault. Because of me, teachers have been patiently writing "easily led" and "cries often" on Missy's report cards for years, and she is still considered a good girl. She won't get braces this year, I think, but she will be all right.

In the next moment two things happen at once. Missy starts to cry, really cry, and my father turns in his seat, looks at me, and then away. It is then that I realize that Missy has decided, without telling me, that straight teeth are not worth eternal damnation. She and Bobby Dunn have confessed, and my father has been called. Now, as he sits with his Bible in his hands and his head bowed, his profile shows none of the cheer of a moment before, and none of the successful-Baptist-preacher expressions I can identify. He does not look spiritual or joyful or weighted down by the burden of God's expectations. He looks furious.

༄༅

There are more announcements than I ever remember hearing on the last night of camp: prayer lists, final volleyball standings, bus departure times, a Lottie Moon Stewardship Award for Denise Meeker. After each item, I forget I have no reason to expect Jesus to help me and I pray for one more; I know that as soon as the last announcement is read, Reverend Stewart will call for a time of personal testimonies before my father's sermon.

Even with my head down I can see Bobby Dunn sinking lower into a center pew and, next to him, Tim Bailey leaning forward, wanting to be first at the microphone. Tim is another of the Bishop School jocks, and he has combed his hair and put on Sunday clothes. In his left hand he is holding my masterwork, reproduced on three-by-five cards. He paid me twenty-five dollars for it — the most I have ever charged — and it is the best piece of my career. The script calls for Tim to talk movingly about meeting God in a car-truck accident near Galveston, when he was ten. In a dramatic touch of which I am especially proud, he seems to imply that God was driving the truck.

Tim, I know, is doing this to impress a Baptist Academy girl who has told him she will go to her cotillion alone before she goes with a boy who doesn't know Jesus as his personal Lord and Savior. He is gripping the notecards as if they were Didi Thornton, and for the first time in a lifetime full of Bible verses, I see an application to my daily living. I truly am about to reap what I have sown.

∞

The announcements end, and Reverend Stewart calls for testimonies. As Tim Bailey rises, so does my father. As he straightens up, he turns again to look at me, and this time he makes a gesture toward the pulpit. It is a mock-gallant motion, the kind I have seen him make to let my mother go first at miniature golf. For an instant that simple reminder that I am not an evil mutant — I have a family that plays miniature golf — makes me think again that everything will be all right. Then I realize what my father is telling me. Tim Bailey will never get to the pulpit to give my testimony. My father will get there first, will tell the worshipers in the packed tent his sorrow and regret over the misdeeds of his little girl. *His little girl.* He is going to do what I have never imagined in all my fantasies about this moment. He is going to forgive me.

Without knowing exactly how it has happened, I am standing up, half running from the choir seats to the pulpit. I get there first, before either my father or Tim, and before Reverend Stewart can even say my name, I give my personal testimony.

I begin by admitting what I have been doing for the past three weeks. I talk about being gripped by hate, unable to appreciate the love of my wonderful parents or of Jesus. I talk about making money from other campers who, in their honest desire to honor the Lord, became trapped in my web of wrongdoing.

Bobby Dunn is crying. To his left I can see Mr. Talliferro; something in his face, intent and unsmiling, makes me relax: I am a Draw. Everyone is with me now. I can hear Missy behind me, still sobbing into her hymnal, and to prove I can make it work, I talk about realizing how blessed I am to have been born within easy reach of God's healing love. I could have been born a Buddhist, I say, and the gratifying gasps from the audience make me certain I can say anything I want now.

For an instant I lose control and begin quoting poetry instead of Scripture. There is a shaky moment when all I can remember is bits of "Stopping by Woods on a Snowy Evening," but I manage to tie the verses back to a point about Christian choices. The puzzled looks on some faces give way to shouts of "Amen!" and as I look out at the rows of people in the green-and-white-striped tent I know I have won. I have written the best testimony anyone at camp has ever given.

I feel, rather than see, my father come to stand beside me, but I do not stop. As I have heard him do hundreds of times, I ask the choir to sing an invitational hymn and begin singing with them, "Softly and tenderly, Jesus is calling, calling to you and to me. Come home, come home. Ye who are weary, come home."

My father never does give a sermon.

While the hymn is still being sung, Bobby Dunn

moves from his pew to the stage, and others follow. They hug me; they say they understand; they say they forgive me. As each one moves on to my father, I can hear him thanking them for their concern and saying, yes, he knows they will be praying for the family.

By ten o'clock, the last knot of worshipers has left the tent, and my father and I are alone on the stage. He is looking at me without speaking; there is no expression on his face that I have seen before. "Daddy," I surprise myself by saying. Daddy is a baby name that I have not used since my ninth birthday. My father raises his left hand and slaps me, hard, on my right cheek. He catches me as I start to fall, and we sit down together on the steps leading from the altar. He uses his handkerchief to clean blood from underneath my eye, where his Baylor ring has opened the skin. As he works the white square of cloth carefully around my face, I hear a sound I have never heard before, and I realize my father is crying. I am crying, too, and the mixture of tears and blood on my face makes it impossible to see him clearly. I reach for him anyway and am only a little surprised when he is there.

Sole Custody

ANNA IS FLYING to Chicago to kidnap her ex-husband Jay's new baby. She didn't know what to pack for this trip — she does not know how long she will be gone or exactly where she will go when she has the child — and the hanging bag she is dragging past the boarding gate to the airplane is swollen with too many sweaters and shoes. When she leaves Dallas on business for her law office, she is a no-nonsense "two dresses, one jacket, two blouses, one skirt" packer who takes pleasure in weaving in and out of more heavily burdened travelers. On the plane, Anna has to ask a young man wearing a baseball jersey to help her lift the bag into the overhead compartment before she sits down, feeling relieved that the evidence that she is not herself today has been safely hidden away. Before she fastens her seat belt, Anna stands up to look around the airplane. The flight isn't crowded for a Friday morning, and she sees only three children, little boys in Sunday suits, the oldest about nine. They must be traveling alone, and as she watches, the oldest reaches across the middle seat to wipe cracker crumbs from around the mouth of the smallest boy. The sweetness of it reaches her from a dozen rows back, and she turns her head. She is glad she has seen the boys so early in the trip, though, since she has learned that it is the unexpected — what she does not see coming — that can pierce her heart.

Since her daughter, Katie, died, Anna has made a routine of this searching-out of the faces of children in public places. She looks directly at them, she registers that they are individual and alive, and she feels protected in some way from the unexpected shocks of recognition that once made it impossible for her to see any child without crying for Katie.

The plane is in the air now, and Anna settles back in her seat. She has not slept more than a few hours since this business with Jay started, four days ago, and she is tempted to let exhaustion take over for the two-hour flight to O'Hare. There will be time later to think about what she is going to do, she decides, and she works her head against the headrest, waiting for sleep to overtake her. She has only a second to prepare herself for the image rising before her. She and Katie are at the kitchen table in the old house on Turtle Creek. It is the summer before Katie got sick, so she is five, and she has come home from nursery school so excited about her discovery of dinosaurs that Anna has to hold her against the over-powering joy of it.

"Slow down, squeaky, I can't understand what you're saying," Anna says when Katie is gathered in her lap.

Katie considers her mother's words; she is all eyes and mouth and impatience. "Mommy, I don't have time," she says, scrambling off Anna's lap in a run. She comes back into the kitchen with scissors and glue and every color of construction paper, and she and Anna make blue dinosaurs instead of dinner.

Anna opens her eyes. She is not going to be able to sleep, and she uncovers her mouth, where one hand has gone automatically at the sight of Katie feeding cheese to a grinning construction-paper beast.

Just over two years have passed since Katie's death, and Anna measures the time that way: two baseball seasons, two birthdays, two rounds of fall school clothes in Sanger's window downtown. There are times when Anna is deliberate in remembering her daughter, when she shuts out the world with no other purpose than to recall some piece of her past with Katie. At other times, thoughts of her daughter are like Muzak in Anna's mind: low-key and familiar but still capable of sudden melodic riffs, like the replay of Katie's voice calling from her bedroom, "Mommy? What can we use for its eyes? I need you, Mommy!"

Anna shakes her head to clear it, because the memories are too strong today and she does not want to think about Katie here, does not want to be a grieving mother reliving the past in a jet somewhere over Oklahoma. She has other things to think about, and she rights herself in the seat until she is sitting the way she does in court.

✥

Kidnapping is the wrong word. Anna has no plans to take the baby — his name is Eli — across state lines. She wants to be clear about this: Jay is the one with delusions, not she; it is only because he has fixed upon Katie as their object that Anna is on this plane.

That she even saw the story Jay wrote for *Chicago* magazine was an accident; it arrived in Monday's office mail from a lawyer friend in Evanston, with a note written across the top: "I know you and Jay aren't in contact anymore, but he told you about this, right?" There was more, but Anna stopped reading, smiling at the phrase "in contact." It had a raffish air to it that she liked, as though she and Jay were two circling small planes whose pilots had decided, on a whim, to switch their radios off. But when she thought about it, it seemed as good a way as any to describe all the things she and Jay weren't to each other anymore. She put the clipping away, but as she worked her way slowly through a stack of depositions, she began to wonder what it was that Jay was supposed to have told her. Finally, she fished it out of the envelope and sat back to read it. This is a joke, she thought, and then, just as quickly, she knew that it was not. "No," she said, so loudly that her secretary, Maryanne, came around the corner to ask what was wrong.

"Nothing. Shut the door," Anna said, and she turned

76

her head before she could see the expression — *Now what's wrong?* — on Maryanne's face.

Alone in her office, she held the story cupped in her hands, feeling its slickness, its lack of weight, and then she began to read. The piece was about the birth of Jay's son, Eli, four months earlier, and Jay's conviction, growing every day, that this happy little boy was Katie, astonishingly alive again in him.

"I will tell you honestly that I had not been a man who believed in God, and after my little girl died there was nothing I believed in at all," Jay had written. "So I do not pretend to know the answers to this miracle that has given me my daughter back again, in a little boy who looks nothing like her but who bears the unmistakable imprint of her soul. I do not need those answers because I have all that matters here with me, in the child my wife Connie and I have given safe passage back into this world."

The story wasn't long, only a page, and as Anna read it again, it shrank even more, until it was only that one paragraph. She read the lines over and over, looking for any suggestion that this was metaphor, that Jay simply meant that Katie lived on in Eli beause any new life is a rebirth. It wasn't there. He meant what he said: Katie had returned to him. Just him. Then Anna read the words out loud, bearing down harder on the personal pronouns each time. *My daughter. My little girl. Here with me. My wife Connie and I.* Then she went back to the beginning and started over, as if it were possible that she had merely overlooked any mention of her as Katie's mother, any acknowledgment that Katie had had a mother at all before she died. Nothing.

When she was done, when she had studied the twelve paragraphs of type as carefully as she would analyze a court brief, she walked down the hall and filled the bathroom sink with cold water. Then she did what Katie had christened "face swimming," holding her hair back with one hand and submerging her face up to the hairline in the basin, feeling the cooling movement of the water all around her. As she did, she saw Katie standing on the beach at Padre Island at high tide, with the straps of her pink bathing suit falling over her shoulders, clapping her hands at the water's retreat. Anna let go of her hair and gripped the basin, so tightly that the color slowly left her hands.

After a long moment, when most of the wildness was gone from her face — when she could say to Maryanne, "Sorry I yelled. It's just the Stanford plea bargain falling apart again" — Anna went back into her office, where pictures of Katie were hung low over the couch, and shut the door. She lay down on the couch and for the first time in years summoned what had once been familiar and dear, not about Katie but about Jay — before Katie got sick, before everything changed. That Jay had had almost no spite, and even less sense of property: he forgave everyone everything, and he let go of anything of his that might be needed elsewhere, secrets as casually as sweaters or bites of ballpark hot dogs. Anna looked at the clipping in her hand. Who was Jay now? She had no idea what the answer was; there simply were no reference points that were of any use to her, nothing in the past that could explain this — the fact that Jay had become a man capable of claiming custody of their only child, living and dead.

She sat up and pulled the Rolodex from the sofa table into her lap. Flipping to the S's, she found the listing for Jay Sawyer and the Chicago number he had given her during the sale of the house. Punching down hard on each number, Anna felt stronger already, as though she were really doing something now and would make sense of all this soon. There was no answer. Anna let the phone ring until the answering machine picked up and a woman's voice said, "Hi. This is 555–9807. Leave your name and number and we'll call you soon. Hope it's a good day for you." At the beep, Anna said, "Jay, call me," and after hesitating a moment added, "It's Anna," and gave her home and work numbers.

Over the next two days, Anna dialed the number every hour and then, when she felt she might choke with all that was going unsaid, every half hour. There was never any answer other than the tape wishing her a good day. "Jay. It's Anna. Call," she said every time, wondering if he would be able to hear in her voice what she saw in her mirror: a woman whose hands trembled, who could not sleep or keep food down, a woman whose memories of her child had been violated by a man she had loved. "Graverobbing," Anna called it on the morning of the third day, and she let the tears come.

When Jay had not called back by Wednesday night, Anna started calling everyone she knew who might know where he was. It was not a long list. Anna had been to Chicago several times on business, but only once with Jay and Katie. Jay had moved there after the separation and divorce; Anna had never met his new wife of a year and did not know who their friends might be. She concentrated instead on calling the few friends from their years together whom she thought Jay might still be in touch with. In five hours on the phone, Anna gathered four invitations to dinner, the possibility of a job in Denver, and the offer of a date for the opera with Jay's old city editor at the *Dallas Morning News.*

When she hung up from the last call, not knowing much more than when she started, except that Connie apparently was a schoolteacher and a blonde, Anna went into the kitchen and made, and then threw away, a tuna sandwich. She stood at the sink for a while, looking out the kitchen window, the way she looked at juries when she didn't know what else to do except remind them that she was a nice woman with a hard job. Usually when she sank to that, some other idea — something else she could do — would come to her fairly quickly, and that happened now. She went back into the living room and called *Chicago* magazine, saying she was an old friend who was coming to town soon and needed to reach Jay.

The girl on the phone — Anna imagined her as a recent college graduate who wrote narrative verse and fantasized about Jay when she was home alone eating Stouffer's — didn't know where Jay was; he wrote for the magazine free-lance, she said, and didn't check in every week. But she did tell Anna that Jay was scheduled to tape the "Chicago Morning" television show that Saturday. When Anna asked, the girl said Jay wouldn't be talking about Eli; it was something else he had written for the magazine, she said — the drug wars on the South Side, maybe? Anna said that sounded right, thanked her, and then, instead of saying good-bye, asked another question.

"Oh," the girl said. "I'm sure you'll get to meet Connie and the baby if you're at the taping. They're always with Jay."

After she hung up the phone, Anna sat for a long time and told herself all the reasons she had to stop here, put all this behind her, and go on, as difficult as that would be. Then she made three more phone calls. The first was to Jay's number, where, again, there was no answer; the second to her office to arrange for a long weekend; and the third to the airline.

❧

The plane begins its descent into O'Hare, and Anna tells herself again that she is doing the right thing. She has had no choice but to make the trip and see the truth for herself. She is sure she knows what the truth is: the baby

81

may have Jay's eyes, as Katie did, or the same long fingers, or her delight in anything musical, but he will have nothing more, because nothing more is possible.

She has no plans for tomorrow morning, other than to get close to Eli for long enough to hold him in her arms. She has no criminal intent, she reminds herself; she is only going to see and then touch Jay's son, nothing more. She is certain it will take only that much to write an end to this appalling postscript to Katie's death and Jay's continuing disintegration; with that done, she will tell Jay exactly what she thinks of his appropriation of Katie for his new life, hand him his son, and go home to Dallas.

The other possibility — that holding Eli in her arms, she will see what Jay sees, believe what he believes — she does not think of at all.

⁂

In the terminal, Anna walks past the people happily reassembling themselves into families, as fast as her hanging bag will allow. She is a hundred yards down the concourse when, to prove that she can, she looks back to see the little boys from the plane run into the arms of a woman about her age. Anna hears the woman calling their names, "Hal! Ken! Michael!" and she starts walking again, faster this time, because she has not been prepared for the sound of a mother's voice after a long separation. She reaches the terminal doors just in time; when tears fill her eyes, it could just be the bright sunlight reflecting off the long line of Yellow Cabs.

"Damn," Anna says, because the Yellow Cabs are orange. The summer Katie was four, and Jay was writing a series about transportation in the year 2000, the three of them took cabs all over the United States on their way to trains and buses and airplanes. Katie loved the fact that all three of them sat together in the backseat, but she never got over her disappointment that Yellow Cabs were usually some other color. Anna had forgotten that, and when she walks down the row of cabs to a blue Town Taxi, there is something in her face that makes the driver especially respectful of her bag. On the Loop, headed for the Palmer House Hotel, Anna takes out a compact and dabs at her eyes until the cabdriver looks less concerned. Then she sits back in her seat and shakes her head, because she does not believe she has been crying over a fleet of misnamed cabs.

All right, she thinks. What if Jay is telling the truth?

"Stop it," Anna says out loud, and the cabdriver looks concerned again and asks if she has changed her mind about the Palmer House. "No," Anna says. "No. I haven't."

He looks at her and then away, as if to say, "Whatever you say, lady," and she laughs. After a moment they are both laughing, and for the rest of the ride she loses herself in a conversation about the 1960s.

At the Palmer House, Anna tips the driver five dollars and goes inside feeling better than she has since she opened her mail on Monday. I'll see the baby and I'll go home, she thinks, and the knowledge that she can do just that — she can end it there — goes with her upstairs to her room. But a few minutes later, unpacking, seeing the indecision she felt in Dallas take shape on the bed in the growing pile of clothes, Anna feels her optimism leave her, all at once, and she sits down.

What am I doing here? she thinks, and then she closes her eyes, the way Katie did when she begged for a scary story and then didn't want to see what might be waiting for her at the end of the hall. Except that Anna doesn't have to conjure up some anonymous bogeyman. She knows exactly what is scaring her; she has already said the words to herself, in the cab.

The truth is that there was a time, when Katie was first sick, when Anna saw the future and knew that her daughter was not just ill, but was dying. And having seen that, how can she be sure Jay's delusion about Eli is only that and nothing more? The answer is that she cannot be sure, and of all the reasons she has to despise Jay, as many reasons as she once had to love him, it is this return of uncertainty about what is possible and impossible that Anna holds against him most.

Anna's vision happened the day after Katie's admission to the hospital, before the lymphoma was diagnosed, on a fall afternoon when all the radios in the children's ward were turned to game five of the World Series. Anna was coming back from the library with an armful of the "big girl" books that Katie took such pleasure in pretending she could read.

The door to the room was half open; when Anna

shifted the books in her arms and used her elbows to push against it, she saw Katie asleep on her back, with her right arm, the one with the IV needle in it, crooked over her head. Anna started to back away — Katie had never been able to sleep on her own before, without her mother or father in the room — but as she did, she looked at the bed again, and this time Katie was dead. There was no other way to say it; Anna looked at her daughter and knew the dripping IV was the cruelest kind of lie, and Katie was gone. At that instant — as Anna reached for the wall and understood that there was no support in the world strong enough for the burden she always would carry now — a smiling nurse pushed past her to wake Katie for her medication, and Anna had her daughter back again.

Thinking about that day in the hospital, Anna walks around her hotel room turning on every light — first the wall switches that control the lighting over the bed and by the window, then the heat lamp in the bathroom, and then the bed, table, and desk lamps. She needs this light to see what she is doing. She is deliberately breaking the rules she set for herself after Katie died, rules that she believes have made it possible for her to wake up in the morning, go downtown to practice law, and come home again at night, all without breaking apart. The rules say she can remember anything about Katie as long as she omits the six months after the first hospital admission, the six months when Katie was dying.

But she cannot deal with tomorrow — cannot make sense of any of this — if she does not think about just that time or, more particularly, Jay and Katie in that time. So, shaking a little because she knows if she starts this, she will have to finish it somehow, Anna reaches for the phone and dials Jay's number again. When there is no answer, only the chirping ring that makes Anna think of Katie chasing crickets on Turtle Creek, she puts the receiver down and walks out of her hotel room.

On the street, Anna waits until another Town Taxi stops for her. She gives the driver Jay's address in Oak Park, and in twenty minutes the cab is in front of a redbrick bungalow. The cabdriver tells Anna where she can catch a bus back to town when she is through, and then he drives away, leaving her alone. It is early evening by now, time for people to be coming home from work, but the street is quiet. Anna has a sudden image of herself standing on the sidewalk in front of Jay's house, and she straightens her suit coat and begins to walk down the driveway to the front porch. The door is painted bright green — the knocker is a brass frog with its legs dangling free — and Anna feels better suddenly, as if this violation of taste were the final proof that Jay is some other person now. She pounds on the door, a little harder than necessary; when no one comes, she walks across the porch to the bay window. The drapes are white gauze — much too thin, Anna thinks — and she has no difficulty seeing into the living room. There are a few pieces of furniture that she recognizes, a loveseat recovered in rose, an oak refectory table, but the dominant decor is classic Couple with Four-Month-Old Baby. There are blankets and stuffed animals strewn everywhere; a huge teddy bear is strapped into a windup swing that Eli is still too young to use. Turning her head, Anna sees that there are pictures arranged in two rows on the far wall. She leans into the window and squints, trying to make the shapes and colors come into focus. She is scanning the top row for the second time, unable to make out either Jay or a baby, when her eyes shift to the pictures arranged below. It takes Anna only a second to realize that every picture there is of Katie.

Anna takes a step back from the window and comes down hard on a squeaky toy shaped like an airplane. She bends down and takes the toy into her hands, cradling it against the cry it makes when touched, and sits down on the porch steps. She is still holding it when she walks away from the house.

The bus lets her off three blocks from the hotel; back in her room, she lays the airplane toy on the table in front of her. She thinks about Jay building a shrine to Katie, in his living room and in his little boy, and she pulls the toy to her. *Katie*, she thinks. *Jay*.

After Anna's vision, in the time it took the nurse to get to Katie's bed by the window, Anna's world shrank to one resolve: *I will not scream.* After a moment, she was able to say in a voice that sounded only a little out of breath, "I'm going to get some coffee while you're with her; I'll be right back."

She walked out of the room and down the hallway, slowly, because she felt as if any sudden movement might bring back the vision of Katie motionless in her bed. In the women's lounge, she went into a stall and waited until the two nurses talking at the sinks had gone. Then she took their place at the mirror, leaning forward to see if her face had changed in any way that would reveal to Katie and Jay what she knew to be true — that the world had undergone so fundamental an alteration as to bring all natural laws into question. She looked tired, nothing more than that, and she understood suddenly that she had entered some new land, where everything looked the same and Katie was dying. The cruelty of it caught her, and before she could stop it, a sound came out of her that she had never heard before. She backed away from the sink, from that sound, into a stall, and sat down, taking in mouthfuls of air against the panic rising in her, concentrating only on letting air out, evenly, slowly, until she was sure she was not going to scream. Then, because there was nothing else she could do, she got up and walked out of the lounge toward Katie's room.

She was there in five minutes, sitting by her child's bed, telling her a story about a princess who had an irritable dolphin for a governess. The story was familiar — if she paused too long, Katie would finish the sentence and go on without her — but Anna had become a different woman, with the same singleness of purpose that she imagined missionaries in the Congo had. Katie was to be her only focus now, since Katie was the only map of any use in both the old world and the new. Several times that afternoon, Anna thought of telling Jay what she had seen — what she now believed was Katie's future — but when he came into the room carrying Katie's bears from home, she looked past him and did not speak. The three of them were in this new land together now — the land made real by her vision, the land where five-year-olds could die — and Anna could not say what the rules were anymore. She could not be sure, but she thought that in this peculiar universe, saying out loud the words "Jay, Katie is going to die" might be exactly the final incantation needed to make it happen. So she kept silent, and in that silence, Anna would come to believe later, two things happened: her marriage to Jay ended, and she became a believer in impossible things, because if Katie could die, what was there of impossibility left in the world?

Two days after her vision, the doctors invited Anna and Jay into a conference room and, using color transparencies for emphasis, told them that while great strides were being made every day, Katie's cancer was incurable. She might live a year, they said, or she might not live three months; everything possible would be done for her, but nothing short of a miracle would save her life. Anna could hear the voices — Jay's rising in disbelief and then rage, the doctors' sympathetic but firm — but she had stopped listening. She already knew that Katie was going to die, and when Jay stopped talking and began to cry, she felt a faint impatience. The feeling was replaced by shame as he reached for her and she accepted his embrace, when all she wanted to do was get away from the conference table, where the slides documenting the probable progression of Katie's disease were spread out like travel brochures. The doctors said again how sorry they were, and then they left; Anna and Jay stayed on at the conference table. Jay was still crying, softly, the way Katie did when she was pushed off a ride at the playground and thought she would never get back on. "Anna," Jay said then, and she thought he was going to tell her they would get through this together, for Katie's sake.

"Anna, Katie's not going to die. I know she isn't," Jay said. He was saying it again when Anna slipped her hands out of his and left the room.

Anna and Jay both took indefinite leaves of absence from their jobs, Anna's as a public defender and Jay's as a political reporter with the *Dallas Morning News,* and made a second home in Katie's corner room at Children's. Looking back, Anna marvels at the ease with which she and Jay separated to take up different orbits around Katie. When they were not tending to her in some way, both did the other things that, incredibly, still had to be done. They ate and made telephone calls; they talked about anything that did not matter; they each took turns staying with Katie while the other went on short walks around the hospital; sometimes they slept or drove home to do laundry at a house that now seemed like a museum of the life they had had together when Katie was well. Anna knew that she — the Anna she had been outside Katie's room that day — seemed not to exist anymore, and certainly the Jay and Anna they had been together were gone, replaced by these people who smiled and played and cried with Katie but were silent and distracted with each other. Some part of Anna knew that she and Jay should be talking more, knew that there must be some comfort they could give each other, but there seemed to be no route she could take to Jay that would not bring her face-to-face with his conviction that Katie was going to live. As much as Anna wanted to believe that, she did not, and the fact that Jay never wavered — even as Katie got sicker every day — created a distance between them that grew until it was itself fully formed, a longer and heavier twin to their dying child. Still, there were times when Anna looked at Jay and wanted her old life back — wanted *him* back — wanted it so badly that her breath left her and she had to swallow, hard, to catch it again. Once she saw Jay watching her and knew he was thinking about her, too. Anna loved him then, but in the next moment they both looked at their daughter, impossibly small in the white hospital bed, and they let each other go. There were other priorities; for the six months it took Katie to die, every act of Anna's was in service to her memory.

I will never forget this, Anna thought every time she rubbed Katie's back, or felt her heart beat when she bent to kiss her good night, or sat up playing Go Fish with her, or held her against the pain that more and more came with daybreak. This is what I will have when Katie is gone.

A hundred times, after Katie was gone, Anna thought that the different ways she and Jay were with each other those last months had to do with Anna's vision in the hospital — with the certain knowledge she had, and Jay did not have, that Katie would die. Anna shamelessly hedged her bets: she bargained endlessly with a God she had not talked to since eighth grade for Katie's life, but every time she touched her or said her name, she was saying good-bye. Jay continued to take no bets at all: he simply never saw Katie's death as a possibility. As Anna watched, he raised denial to greater heights each day, until at the funeral he looked sick not so much with grief as with some awful surprise. When Jay held Katie or kissed her, he was not saying, as Anna was, I will not forget this. He was saying, I can throw this moment away. We will have years of other moments.

When it was too late, on the day Katie went into a coma from which she did not wake, Anna looked up and saw, really saw, Jay. He was leaning over Katie's bed, his left hand stretched out around the tubes and oxygen mask to stroke her hair back from her forehead. "Come on, squeaky," he was saying. "It's a beautiful day, and Daddy's here. Open your eyes, baby. Let Daddy see you."

There was more — Jay never stopped talking as he smoothed Katie's hair over and over — but Anna could not listen. She went out into the hall and leaned against the wall, closing her eyes against the image of Jay still alive to hope, when there was no hope. And for the first time, Anna realized what it would mean to Jay, after Katie was dead, that he had never said good-bye. She felt dazed, as though she had come out of the dark into sunlight so bright it hurt to see it. "Jay," she said, and she felt a tug of recognition that propelled her back into Katie's room. She walked toward Jay, still at Katie's bed; she could not save Katie, she knew that, but she could try to save Jay. She could make him save himself.

"Jay," she said again, but he did not turn to look at her, and he shook off the hand she reached out to him.

"I'm talking to Katie now, Anna," he said. And then, without pausing, "Where were we, baby? Oh, well, when I was little, we all rode horses on Saturday morning, but my horse was the best. You'll have a horse when you're bigger, not next year, next year you'll still be too small, but the year after that, for sure."

"Jay," Anna said again, and when he did not respond, she went back into the hall and wept for them all. She knew then that she was going to lose them both, but she went on doing what there was to do. She sat by Katie's bed, listening to the *eek! eek!* the portable life-support

93

system made as it took each breath for her; she tried again to talk to Jay. But in the end, she stopped trying, because she did not have any energy to spare for anything but the task of gathering her memories. If that was the only way she could keep Katie with her, she must have them all. By then, Anna knew that memories were the only thing she would be able to salvage.

She was right about that, too. Four months after Katie's death, Jay moved out of the house, and six months after that, the divorce was final. Anna signed the papers dated Sept. 8, 1986, but she knew that other dates mattered more: the day Katie came in from the backyard complaining that her stomach hurt; the day she decided not to share her vision with Jay; the day she stopped trying to make Jay face the truth and take leave of his child; and, finally, the day Katie died. When she was gone, when Jay was made to see that all the hope and bravado had brought him nothing, he blamed Anna.

"You knew she was going to die," he screamed at her before he left, and Anna closed her eyes and saw Katie clearly, wearing a red pompom hat and curling her tongue at a nurse holding a tray. Her mind full of Katie, she did not have to hear Jay shout at her or the front door slam or the car pull out of the driveway. Most of all, she did not have to hear the indictment behind the words: You believed in her death, and Katie died. What would have happened if both of us had believed in her life?

꩜

The clock by Anna's bed reads five after midnight when she has remembered it all, and she stands up to turn off the same lights she turned on three hours ago. She is thinking still about the day Jay left the house, about the way he blamed her for what he saw as her easier acceptance of Katie's death. If she sees him tomorrow, she thinks, she will say what she never did in the months after Katie's funeral: "Children aren't like Tinker Bell, Jay; wishing doesn't make them live."

Not "if" she sees him, she thinks then; "when." She will see Jay tomorrow, Jay and Eli, and she will see for herself what is true and what is not. She stops by the table and dials Jay's number again; he answers on the third ring.

"Hello," he says. "Hello. Who is this?" Anna has not heard his voice in more than a year, and she stands for a moment listening before she replaces the receiver. She will talk to Jay tomorrow.

In bed, Anna lies with the curtains open wide enough for her to see the lights of the Sears Tower. She has never run a marathon, but she imagines that this is how racers feel coming down the top of a hill toward the finish line. She is drained — she wants to get a glass of water but stays where she is, too tired to move — but she feels good, too. She has remembered Katie and Jay, and she has not fallen apart. And she knows what she is going to do next. Waiting for sleep, Anna sees for the first time how zealously she has regulated her memories of Katie in the years since her death: shaping their content,

95

guarding against unwanted appearances by other characters like Jay or the doctors with the color slides, even selecting the times when it is "appropriate" to remember. How sad, Anna thinks, and she is surprised at the choice of words, since she has only been protecting herself against more pain.

Some choices, though, have not been Anna's to make; some things she believed she would never forget, she has forgotten. Katie would have been seven this year — Anna believes she would be wearing her hair in a braid and taking piano — but Anna can no longer get a precise picture of her face when she closes her eyes. She can remember so much: colors, physical sensations, smells, sounds — Katie's skin, like a baby seal's, wet and taut, when she was laid on Anna's belly after her birth; her laugh; her hair after a bath; the unholy joy in her eyes the day she discovered the "music" toilets make when flushed; tears standing on her eyelashes. But she cannot make her child's face come into focus. The image is unmistakably Katie, but it is indistinct, soft, without edges or depth. Anna is almost asleep now — she can feel herself being pulled down into darkness — but she is still thinking about Katie's face and the fact that she must look at pictures to see it exactly. For an instant, a panicked thought pushes sleep away: Will I know when I hold Eli? Will I know if it's Katie? Anna digs her body further into the perfumed sheets, taking deep breaths to quiet herself. I'll know, she thinks, and she carries that with her into the night.

৩৯৫

Anna wakes to another truth, a truth that is with her as she fumbles for the light and sits up in bed: she loved Katie, oh, God, so much, and Katie loved her. But Katie was Jay's, too. Anna pulls her knees to her chest, wanting to feel any kind of human warmth close to her. She takes a deep breath and lets it go, letting the truth escape with it into the hotel room. Katie loved Jay best. It started when Anna was still pregnant, when Jay would go out for orange juice for Saturday breakfasts and came home instead with toys — odd, enchanting toys — for the baby he somehow knew was a girl. When Katie was born, Jay behaved just as he did when he found the elusive single piece needed to make a big story work: he was simply, blissfully, happy, and in those days he was always smiling. Anna tightens her grip on her knees because none of these memories is safe.

Anna's memories are different. In those memories, loving experiments with action and sound and dialogue, it's she and Katie who made the construction-paper dinosaur. Anna can see it clearly, Katie hunched over the kitchen table with a blue crayon, coloring in the eyes, saying, "How do I make eyelashes, Mommy? How do we make its eyes?" It happened; Anna knows that. Jay and Katie told her about it when they met her at the door one Saturday with a sequined brontosaurus. It was

Jay whose hand guided the scissors Katie held, Jay who made a Styrofoam tail a foot long, Jay for whom Katie named the creature.

Anna's memories are lies and not lies, and now, sitting up in the Palmer House double bed, she acknowledges that. She has done what she had to do: she has taken some of Jay's memories of Katie as her own. After the funeral, when she and Jay went back to the house, where there was no air that Anna could breathe without gasping, she realized that in every memory she had stored so carefully of Katie, she was dying. She screamed at Jay, "Help me; I can't see Katie's face," and he looked at her for a long moment before he helped her into bed. "She loved me," she said to Jay when he bent to cover her with a quilt.

"Of course she did" was all he said. That night, he moved into the guest bedroom, and Anna could not bring herself to go to him. After a while, she no longer wanted to. She had her memories.

In the morning, there are no ghosts in the room that Anna can see. She orders room-service orange juice and eggs and sits reading the *Chicago Tribune* until it's time to leave for the network affiliate where the show is being taped. She walks out of the hotel onto Michigan Avenue and turns left toward Water Tower Place. She knows where she is going, and she walks quickly, shivering a little against the North Shore wind. At the television station, she stands in line with other men and women waiting to go upstairs to the taping. Twice she hears Jay's name and turns around, but it's only neighborhood activists talking about his interview with a fourteen-year-old crack dealer. When the elevator comes, Anna is the first one on; on the sixteenth floor, she gets off last and lags behind in the corridor as the ushers show the audience members to their seats. Suddenly Anna feels ridiculous, not like a lawyer or even a wronged woman but simply like a person who gets caught making up stories. What is she going to do here? She has put her energy into the revision of her personal history; when she has thought of this place at all, she has imagined Jay and Connie and Eli in plain sight, waiting for her. Now she's here, and they are nowhere to be seen.

"I loved my daughter," Anna says aloud, and she feels something give inside her because this is true. She knows it is. People are looking at her now, but she does what she does in court: she picks one face, a woman about her own age wearing a Take Back the Night! T-shirt, and talks directly to her.

"She died, and I tried to keep her with me anyway. I didn't want to share her with anyone. But she's gone. Katie's gone."

People are moving away from her, wondering in low voices what to do, but the woman Anna is speaking to does not back away. She takes Anna's hands and holds them in hers, tightly, the way Katie held the "fairies" they captured on summer nights on the front lawn. Anna is crying now because she remembers that. On hot nights after dinner, she and Katie would take their iced tea to the front porch, and Anna would make up stories about fairies who lived in trees and only came down for the best little girls.

"Make one come, Mommy," Katie would say, and then Anna would clap her hands and push them gently on top of Katie's fists.

"There's one, baby," Anna would say every time, and every time Katie would echo, "There's one."

Anna is crying harder now, because how can she not have remembered that? The woman holding her hands begins to walk backward, pulling Anna along toward a bench beside the elevator.

"Do you have a little girl?" Anna asks, and the woman nods yes, her own eyes filling with tears. "I'm glad," Anna says. "Thank you for helping me. I'm all right now. I just remembered something, is all."

She pulls her hands free and takes the tissues the woman is offering. She blows her nose, a horrible wet sound that makes her laugh, and she thinks about Jay and Connie and Eli. Behind her, in the studio, the taping has begun, and she can hear Jay's voice laying down the law about murder in the streets. She says thank you again to the woman who has helped her, and then she walks to the studio door and looks through the square of glass. The stage and the seats are at a right angle to where she is standing; she can see Jay and, in the front row, the top half of a woman in a jogging suit, holding a baby in her arms. But Anna does not go forward into the studio; she turns around and walks to the elevator and then into the street. Somewhere near here is the park where she taught Katie to hopscotch, that August day when the two of them went for a walk together, leaving Jay to ride cabs around the city by himself. At the first stoplight on Michigan Avenue, Anna hesitates for a moment because she is not sure whether the park is uptown from the art museum or downtown. She is not worried, though; she crosses with the light and moves quickly through the midmorning crowd on the sidewalk, knowing that with time she will remember everything.

A Morning in the Late Cretaceous Period

EMILY'S HUSBAND, Tom, has been planning this trip to opening day of the new dinosaur exhibit at the St. Paul Science Museum for weeks, but they aren't past the gift shop when he abandons all interest in any vertebrate but Emily. He is following her up and down the dinosaur trail, trying to extract from her a complete list of behaviors she would find unforgivable in a loved one. She stops speaking to him halfway through the Triassic period, feigning desperate interest in the museum dioramas of earth 225 million years before, but he steps closer to her and raises his voice. Emily knows where this is going, and she walks faster, wondering why Tom has never told her whether dinosaurs mated for life, whether love and monogamy were any part of what endangered them.

"What about white-collar crime? What if I bilk a church out of a million dollars, but it's a big Episcopal church downtown and I give all the money to homeless people? Will you forgive me?"

"Hush," Emily says.

"Okay, I'm Oliver North and you're my wife; you're home alone one night watching 'Nightline' and you realize I'm guilty as sin. What do you do?"

"I call up Ted Koppel and ask him out."

"I'm serious. I'm Oliver North; are you going to forgive me?"

"You know, Ted and I have only been waiting for you to go crazy before we start dating."

"Forget about Oliver North, then; let's say we pin down something you think is unforgivable, and then I have some sort of breakdown and I go right out tomorrow and do it. But then I'm sorry, and I want to spend the rest of my life making it up to you. Are you going to give me another chance, or not?"

A Cub Scout pack taking the same route through the museum fans out to walk around them, all but the two den mothers, whom Emily has seen elbowing each other for the past fifty million years, taking in every word Tom says. She makes a face at them, and they hurry past.

"I'll tell you what I'll do," she says. "I'll forgive you for ruining our Sunday if you'll just stop this. I mean it; I don't want you to do this anymore."

"So you'll forgive me if I do what you want? That doesn't leave me much room to screw up, does it?"

Emily walks away; Tom grabs for her arm, but she shakes his hand loose and keeps moving, through the green and lovely landscape of the beginning of the world: ferns, conifers, ginkgoes, and a herd of tiny dinosaurs, not one of them bigger than an individual Cub Scout. Emily stops, leaning into the display to get a closer look, and hears Tom behind her, reciting little-known facts about the compsognathus. She doesn't look at him; she is reevaluating the beginning of the world. Examined closely, it looks makeshift and worn. The dinosaurs' skin is shiny, patched in places like cheap upholstery, and the greenery is mostly felt and papier-mâché. She starts to poke Tom, to see if he's noticed it, too, and remembers that there's trouble in faux paradise. She dodges his hand again and walks on.

They enter the Cretaceous period. All around them, the known world is splitting into separate continents, and Emily pushes ahead, until she's standing alone somewhere on the edge of North America.

After a moment, Tom comes toward her, slowly, across Africa and then Asia. "I just want to know where I stand," he says. "All I'm asking for is some idea of what you'll forgive and what you won't. If we get the categories straight, we won't find out later that I've just done something you think is unforgivable."

"Like my first husband did, you mean?" Emily asks. "That's what you want, isn't it? To know you won't end up like Jimmy? How can I answer that?"

"You can tell me what he did." There is on Tom's face, still, a solemn expression of scientific inquiry, of seeking-after-truth; it disappears when she pushes him, hard, with both hands. He falls backward into the earth, where dinosaurs are dying from the weight of their own history, and Emily steps off North America without looking down, into the wide, carpeted sea.

❧

On Saturday morning, when Emily came downstairs, Tom was sitting at the kitchen table, transferring the schedule for their big weekend from the wall calendar to his datebook. He'd planned these two days so carefully that he had even named them: the squares for October 5 and 6 on the Earth First calendar said "Dinosaur Days" in his tiny up-and-down script. He had made the notation weeks ahead, and Emily never looked at it without thinking of a high school prom gone horribly wrong: couples slow-dancing in a Catholic-school gym decorated to look like the dawn of time. She kept the joke to herself and smiled every time Tom went back to the calendar to add other activities to Dinosaur Days. She could take prehistoric creatures or she could leave them alone, but she loved that Tom couldn't, that he'd arranged his life, down to becoming a geologist and a steadfast, meticulous adult, all around a boy's dream of the past.

Before Tom, the men in Emily's life had been careless, with a talent for rash acts but none at all for remorse. And Emily had mirrored them. Outwardly, she was what her mother still called a good girl: she kept up appearances; she was kind when kindness cost her nothing; she was careful about not getting caught. But in her own heart, she knew herself to be feckless, with no purpose much beyond getting to the next week and the next entanglement. She never said the words out loud to Tom, but she believed that he had made possible the woman she'd become, like the fairy-tale woodsman whose touch coaxes the live girl out of the oak tree.

"The co-op first, to buy what we need for the picnic lunch after the museum tomorrow," Tom said, "and then we'll have a late breakfast at Bruno's, okay?"

Emily nodded, pretending not to know that the schedule said "Sat: Co-op/Picnic Food. Brkfst/Brunos."

There weren't any parking spaces at Seward Co-op. There never were any on Saturday mornings, but Tom drove into the lot and looked for one anyway, while Emily sat quietly and waited for him to give up — except he never gave up. He drove up the Entrance Only row whistling, waving at people in their cars who might have been leaving but weren't, and then turned to drive down the Exit row. On the fifth go-round, just as Emily was framing a wifely comment about all the parking twenty yards away on the street, a red Volvo backed out of a corner space, and Tom was in. "Got it," he said, exactly as though this parking space, and no other, comprised the last piece of his happiness. He looked over at Emily then, smiling, and she made an idiotic thumbs-up gesture back at him. She and Tom had been married for two years, but small things about him, his hopefulness especially, could still disarm her completely.

Inside the co-op door, Tom went left, for the *Times* and bagels, and Emily got a cart. She was in the produce aisle, reaching for an eggplant at the back of the bin, when she heard a voice behind her, calling her name. She had only enough time to realize it wasn't Tom before she turned and saw a man walking toward her, grinning, with a head of Chinese cabbage in each hand.

Emily recognized the Fair Isle sweater he was wearing a second before she recognized her ex-husband, which was understandable: the sweater, handmade by her, didn't seem to have changed, and Jimmy had. He looked happy and fit; more than that, he looked as though he had never been unhappy or unfit. Watching him, Emily was amazed. Everything about him spoke health and possibility, as though nothing better could happen to a man out for a morning stroll with his cabbages than to run into his ex-wife.

Hundreds of times in the past Emily had imagined seeing Jimmy again, but in her fantasies only the settings ever changed, from hospital wards to soup kitchens to jail cells. Jimmy himself never changed — that was the point, that he would never grow up, never get better — and now, as he came closer, Emily felt cheated all over again. She wanted Tom; she could see the top of his head at the back of the store, and she wished for him, as though the strength of her longing alone could make him materialize next to her. She felt sick and closed her eyes like a child; when she opened them, Jimmy was there.

"Emily, this is great, running into you. I said to Caroline on the way over that you used to come here all the time. Didn't I, Caroline?" he said over his shoulder. "Honey, this is Emily."

The woman who'd joined them was as tall as Jimmy and, Emily thought, a fairly recent high school graduate. She held out her hand, and Emily had to overcome the urge to look at it before she took it.

"I'm Caroline Swann," she said, and Emily answered, "It's nice to meet you; hello, Jimmy." The words were automatic, and she didn't listen to herself say them; she was praying for Tom, and at the same time she was thinking, Bingo! because Jimmy hadn't gotten this healthy on his own. He'd married this woman — this young, young woman — to do it.

"James talks about this place, about how you always shopped here but he wouldn't eat anything from a health-food store," Caroline said. "He's really turned around on that one; we're opening our own bakery in Cedar-Riverside, and he makes the most wonderful whole-grain bread."

Emily didn't believe it, but she was still back on "James."

"Jimmy bakes bread?" she said.

"No one calls me Jimmy anymore," he said, stepping closer to her. He hadn't put either cabbage in Caroline's basket, and for a moment Emily was sure he was going to hand one of them to her as a kind of consolation prize. Instead, he pointed toward her, and she felt the cabbage leaves, cool and damp, on the inside of her wrist. "It's been five years."

"Five whole years," Emily said. Jimmy continued to smile, but Caroline took a half step forward, until she was standing a little in front of him.

Emily was opening her mouth to say good-bye, or something more permanent, when a dozen bagels fell into her cart. She felt Tom's arm around her waist and looked up at him; he was smiling, too, already taking the hand Jimmy was offering.

She ducked her head at the picture the four of them made, and heard, as if from some distance, Jimmy explaining to Tom who he was, who Caroline was, how they had moved back to the Twin Cities from Iowa, and how lucky it was that they had run into Emily.

Jimmy talked, and Emily looked at Tom, hoping to see that her second husband loathed her first by instinct, but he was laughing at Jimmy's description of "yeast-heads," customers who had a serious two-loaf-a-day habit. They were all laughing, Caroline the hardest, and Emily wished, dispassionately, for one of Tom's tyrannosaurs to lay waste to Seward Co-op, not even sparing the sweet kids in the back who made yogurt. That she had told Tom about her first marriage only in the barest outline form — deliberately stripped of drama, even of interest — was no excuse; he had no business liking Jimmy.

"Emily teaches first grade now," Tom was saying. "That's how we met; she was finishing up at the U, and I spoke to a class about how to help children understand dinosaurs."

"She's always been smart," Jimmy said, and before Emily could say anything, both men smiled, not at her but at some knowledge they shared.

"We have to go," Emily said over Tom, who had started in on their plans for the weekend, talking up the museum exhibit to Jimmy and Caroline. He stopped in midsentence, and Emily saw him register, much too late, that something was wrong. "I didn't realize what time it was," she said. "We really have to get going."

Jimmy and Caroline looked at each other; it was a married look, full of complicity and affection, and Emily turned away from it.

"Wait," Jimmy said. "Please."

His face had changed. Emily thought that the glow was still there, but dimmer, as though somewhere a switch had been thrown. "Can we talk for a minute?" he said. "I mean sit down and talk? It won't take long, I promise."

Emily wanted to run; she wanted to shake Caroline's hand free of Jimmy with some awful warning; she wanted Dinosaur Days to go according to schedule, beginning in the half-light of early morning, when she had kissed Tom awake and been so sure that her brief history with him was all she had to concede.

"No," she said. "We can't. Tom, let's go."

"I just have two things to say. That's all," Jimmy said, and he didn't wait for her to agree. He began, "I," and stopped. Caroline stage-whispered, "Go on." It was the whisper that held Emily in place, facing Jimmy, waiting.

"I don't drink anymore," he said. "That's the main thing. The other is that I've been going back to people who knew me when I was drunk, so I can take responsibility for what I did to them. Caroline and I have been talking about finding you since we came back to Minneapolis. We were just saying this morning that it was time, and then I looked up and there you were.

"There's a lot I could say, but what it comes down to is that I know how much I hurt you, and I'm sorry. I really am, Emily."

Caroline said softly, "Oh, James," at the same moment Emily said, "That's three things," and was rewarded with her first glimpse of the old Jimmy, in the flush starting above his sweater.

"What?" he said.

"You said *two* things; that's three."

"Em," Tom said.

"No," she said, and this time she did run, not even waiting to see if one husband, or two, were behind her. At the checkout line nearest the exit, she edged past a woman in a camouflage vest and then realized she was still holding the eggplant. She turned around, wanting someplace to put it down, but the checkout counter was covered with sacks of rice. All Emily could think about was Jimmy and Caroline somewhere behind her, advancing from the rear of the store, holding hands and making amends. Finally, she said, "Excuse me," and shoved the eggplant into an empty rack labeled *Prevention Magazine.*

The woman in camouflage made a shocked sound, but Emily didn't stop; she was already in the car when Tom opened the driver's-side door and got in.

"Are you all right? James seemed very concerned about you. I think he and Caroline thought you'd be glad to hear he's sorry."

"Jimmy. His name is Jimmy."

Tom moved to start the car and then sat back. "I wish I'd realized in the co-op how upset you were. He really hurt you, didn't he?"

"If we're going to eat breakfast at Bruno's, we need to go. Please, let's just go; I don't want to talk here." She was quiet until they were halfway down University to the restaurant, when Tom sighed, a little sound he covered with a cough. "You were in there long enough after I left," she said. "What were you doing, exchanging phone numbers with your new friends?" Her voice was unrecognizable, but she had seen the look on Tom's face before, in the dinosaur fields of Colorado the past summer, when something thought to be precious — a bone fragment, a bit of fossil — turned out to be only ordinary, after all.

There was a 7-Eleven on the right; Tom pulled into the parking lot and positioned the car carefully, backing up a couple of times to fit exactly within the lines, before he turned to face her. "Em, tell me what's wrong. In the whole time we've known each other, all you've said about James Swann — excuse me, Jimmy — is that you were only married a year. What did he do to you?"

"I need something cold to drink. Are you coming in?" When he didn't move, she opened the car door. "Can we talk about it in a minute? I need a little time."

Tom followed her into the store. Emily was waiting in line with her bottled water when a young Vietnamese girl behind her dropped a paper cup, splattering Emily's legs with coffee and splotches of powdery cream. Tom came toward her, holding out his handkerchief, but it was the Vietnamese girl who took it. She bent down and wiped the coffee away; Emily tried to pull free, but the girl wouldn't let her go. She kept on dabbing at Emily's legs, making little sounds of concern.

When she was done, she stood up and gave the dripping handkerchief back to Tom. "I'm so sorry," she said to Emily. "Please forgive me. I didn't mean to hurt you."

Emily started to tell her not to worry, that everything was all right, but a new tightness in Tom's face caused the words to catch high in her throat. Emily nodded several times, hoping the gesture meant something, and walked out of the store.

Tom stayed behind, talking to the girl, and Emily supposed he had taken over the task of explaining. She watched him through the storefront and said, "I forgive you," into the silence, over and over, varying the speed and pitch, the tone and intensity, nodding her head in time to the rhythm and language of absolution.

When Tom got into the car, she took her drink from him and gulped it, wanting to fill up the space where the words had been only a moment before. When she was done, she looked at him. Whatever had shown on his face in the store was gone; he seemed concerned, nothing more.

"Are you all right?" he asked again, and she said yes, not wanting to talk until the drive was over and they were sitting at a table in the back of Bruno's, where the low windows overlooked the Mississippi.

"I wish I'd known enough to get you out of there," Tom said when the waiter was gone. "I wouldn't have stood there talking to him like nothing was wrong."

"It's not your fault. It was just hard seeing him."

"What happened when you two were married?"

"You heard him say he hurt me." Emily knew as she said the words that they were both answer and evasion, truth and lie, an indictment of Jimmy that left her own guilt out of it. She was surprised, all over again, at how much she wanted it that way.

"Why'd you marry him?"

"Why do you marry anybody?" she said, and she saw Tom flinch. She reached for his hand. "I loved him. I don't like talking about it; it was so long ago."

Tom nodded, and Emily believed for the first time that the encounter with Jimmy could be contained: it had happened but was over, exactly as their marriage was over; it had nothing to do with her now. She believed it until the next morning, when she and Tom walked into the museum together; she was standing alone, waiting for him to come back with their tickets, when she saw him watching her, the way he had done at the 7-Eleven, as though he were checking what he saw against a list in his head. She knew, even before he asked the first question about what she would and would not forgive, that she had been wrong to think she was safe.

Tom lands at the foot of a ginkgo tree, and Emily's path to him is blocked by Cub Scouts running to offer first aid. She waits where she is; she can't look at Tom, but she can hear him, patiently explaining why he doesn't need a Band-Aid or some Absorbine Junior. She cups her hands over her face; the breath on her fingers is panicky, fast and hot. The den mothers arrive to shoo the boys away, returning once for stragglers, and still Emily stays in place.

When she can't hear the Scouts anymore, she lifts her hands; Tom's head is down, and he doesn't move to stand up. Emily has an idea now that he will never get up, that she has moved her marriage toward extinction with an act she can't explain and can't take back. She walks to him and leans down to talk softly, so that no one else can hear.

"Tom, please, I'm sorry; I didn't mean to hurt you. Please get up, and we'll go somewhere and talk."

A museum security guard is walking toward them. When he is halfway there, Tom rolls forward onto his knees and then pulls himself all the way up. "I fell," he says to the guard, who is examining the ginkgo for damage. When he doesn't find any, he waves them away, and Tom walks past Emily without a word.

He gets to the parking ramp first. Emily hurries to catch up, certain that he's going to leave her, but he is waiting when she gets to the car.

"I can't believe I pushed you," she says. "I can't believe this is happening."

He holds up a hand, a scientist ordering the elements. "What did Jimmy do?"

"I'll tell you if that's what you want. I just wish you'd believe me that it doesn't have anything to with you and me. It was so long ago."

"Why can't you forgive him, then?"

Emily doesn't answer right away; she's thinking about how to say it when Tom opens the car door.

"I'm going back to the exhibit and then to the office for a while. I'll take the bus home." He is gone before she can stop him, and she concentrates on moving into the driver's seat, giving herself no time to turn the other way and watch him leave her.

At home, Emily works on lesson plans at the kitchen table, stopping every few minutes to look at, but not pick up, the telephone. When Tom isn't home for dinner, she goes into the den and sits at his desk to call his office number. He answers on the first ring, and Emily can hear the effort in his voice; he is willing to be civil, it seems, but not to come home to her.

She says again how sorry she is and then tells him

117

she's going to bed early, exhausted, and to please not call before he leaves the office. They talk for a few more minutes, until Tom says, "Good night, Em," almost normally, and she feels a small surge of hope that disappears as quickly as it comes.

In the hallway, Emily resets the answering machine to pick up on the first ring and goes out the kitchen door to the garage. She tells herself she can do this only if she does it quickly; she takes I-94 the seven miles to Minneapolis, rolling down the windows and cranking up the radio, changing lanes whenever another car slows her progress. At the Cedar-Riverside exit, she takes a breath and slows down because she only knows the general area, not an address. She drives up Cedar and then turns around; halfway down the street, on the right, she sees it: a blue-and-white-striped awning above a tiny storefront wedged between the movie house and the mountaineering store.

Everything's closed. Emily pulls into a space in front of the movie house and sits for a moment, shifting in her seat to look behind her, at Swann's Bakery. She gets out of the car and walks toward it. The front window is dark, but as she steps close to it, cupping her hands to her face to look inside, she sees a thin string of light moving forward from behind a curtain at the back of the store. She thinks that if she taps hard on the window, the curtain will be pushed aside, and she'll see Jimmy and Caroline, gathered in their own light, baking the next day's bread. She is tired and cold, and when she moves, it is away from the window, toward her car. She was right about one thing, she thinks: the Jimmy who is healthy and happy has nothing to do with her.

At the house, Emily goes upstairs to the bedroom. She takes off the jeans and T-shirt she's worn all day and goes into the bathroom, where she stands in the shower for twenty minutes under water that is almost too hot to bear.

Out of the shower, she takes the white Sierra Club T-shirt she sleeps in from the wardrobe's bottom shelf and unfolds it on the cherrywood bed that belonged to her grandmother. The shirt is an early artifact of her history with Tom. He gave it to her on their wedding trip to the Rocky Mountains, along with a completely unexpected speech about wanting to give her the earth, and all the time they were in Colorado, she wore it underneath her other clothes, next to her skin, feeling light-headed as her other history emptied out of her. She gladly let the past go; in the mountains everything she did was for the first time, and all the while she was discarding memories of herself with Jimmy, with any man who was not Tom.

She holds the shirt for a long time, fingering the mountain emblem, the raised lettering, the faint constellation of spaghetti sauce on the left shoulder, and then puts it back on the shelf. She takes out a bra and panties and puts them on before she goes back into the bathroom for makeup: foundation, eyeliner, mascara, blush, lipliner, lipstick. She almost never wears anything but

119

lipstick anymore; when she looks in the mirror, she's squinting from the effort to concentrate. Finished, she bows her head, avoiding the mirror altogether.

In the bedroom, she goes to the wardrobe again and begins pushing clothes to one side to find what she wants. She reaches to the very back and comes out with a straight black skirt and a fuzzy red sweater. The clothes are bright and cheap, the kind of thing Jimmy liked her to wear. Emily lays them on the bed and makes a circle of the room, gathering in her arms everything else she will need: black hose, slip, black heels.

When she is dressed, she hesitates again, but only for a moment; she's thinking not of stopping but of being done with it. She turns off the overhead light and the room's two lamps. In darkness, using her hands to edge along the outlines of furniture, she walks to the bed. She pulls at the quilt and pillows, without seeing them, and lies down on her back in the tangle of bedclothes; she stays like that, motionless, until she is ready. She breathes in and moves to arrange her body: knees slightly raised, left arm above her head, right arm straight out, fingers curled and pressed into the bed, as though held there by a greater weight. When she has it right, when she is in the exact posture of the stranger she saw Jimmy making love to in this bed, she opens her eyes and stares at the ceiling, unblinking, until she has no choice but to let tears fill her eyes. When she cries, when she feels the tears running down her cheeks to her neck for the last time, dampening the red fuzz of the sweater, she's done.

∾

Emily wakes in darkness. She is facedown on the bed, tangled in the quilt, and she struggles to reach the light and turn around, to see if Tom has come home. She knows the answer before her hand closes on the lamp: she's alone.

She gets up too fast, not stopping to separate dizziness from panic, and goes downstairs. In the kitchen, she stops to think about what to do, whether to call the office again or get in the car and go there, or wherever else she can think of that Tom might be. She is sitting on the edge of the kitchen table, and when she looks up, in the direction of the car, she sees the calendar. A neat black line has been drawn through Dinosaur Days.

"Tom?" she says. "Where are you?"

She begins to search for him, approaching each room in the house like a child in the dark, sliding across the hardwood floors, holding her breath until the moment when the lights come on. He is nowhere in the house, not in the living room, or the den, or the garage, or any of the rooms upstairs. She is starting back to the living room to begin the hopeless circuit again when she thinks of the backyard. She turns on the patio lights and sees Tom, sitting in a deck chair at the far end of the rock garden they built together. The chair is turned away from the house, and she doesn't call to him. She walks toward the garden, dragging another chair, still in the clothes she wore for Jimmy.

When she's a few steps away, Tom speaks to her, without turning around. "I was going to come in, but it's nice out here," he says, and she can't tell if it's un-happiness or exhaustion that thins his voice, making it fade in and out like the voices in dreams.

She unfolds her chair next to his; they've sat out on the lawn before, many times, and for a moment Emily lets herself believe they are here only to view the stars at the close of Dinosaur Days. She makes herself stop, thinking that all the promise of the beginning of the world has come to this, love that cannot ensure happi-ness, and the face she turns to Tom is shaken, on the edge of tears. "I'm glad you're home," she says. "I was worried about you. Are you okay?"

"I'm not sure. I don't think so."

They are in the shadow of the patio lights, and Emily sees Tom taking in for the first time what she's wearing. She's forgotten the clothes, and now she looks down at them; she is unfamiliar, like a memory she and Tom do not share, and she shifts in her chair, wanting him to see her clearly.

"I used to wear these clothes when I was with Jimmy. I put them on tonight to remember what it was like."

"Em," Tom says. "Maybe you were right; maybe tell-ing me now won't help anything."

"Are you saying you don't want to hear it?"

"I want this to be over, I know that."

"Then listen to me," Emily says, and then she stops, unsure even now that she can say this out loud. "I loved Jimmy. I wanted him to stop drinking, but I didn't think about leaving. I loved him.

"A lot of things happened; he got sick and lost his job, and he took some money from his parents and didn't tell me. They quit seeing him, and he promised to stop drinking, for me, to make me happy. I thought I'd cured him. Then I came home from school late, after dinner, and he was in bed with a friend of his sister's."

"Oh, honey," Tom says. She feels his hope even then, his conviction that the worst is over. "I knew it had to be something like that. I shouldn't have kept after you to tell me, but I couldn't stop thinking that I had to know why you couldn't forgive him. I had to be sure I wouldn't do whatever it was. You know I won't, don't you?"

"I know. But that's not what I have to tell you. That's the part that doesn't matter anymore; what matters is what I did." He looks at her, not understanding. "I've never told anyone this."

"Emily, wait. You don't have to tell me."

"You're going to forgive me, aren't you?" She sees his shoulders drop, feels the heart go out of him, and doesn't wait for him to answer.

"I left when I saw them that night, and went to a friend's house. Jimmy was drunk, almost passed-out, and he didn't come after me. I didn't go back for two days, and when I did, he wasn't there. Just Sanka was there."

She expects Tom to say "Sanka?" but he doesn't; he is quiet, waiting for the rest of it.

"I got him at the animal shelter for Jimmy's birthday; he was a black Lab puppy, four months old and not very smart. He liked me okay, but from the start he loved Jimmy. Jimmy gave him beer."

Tom hasn't moved; Emily listens for his breathing but can only hear her own.

"I had to drag Sanka outside because he didn't want to leave the house without Jimmy, but when he saw the car, he jumped right in. I drove to Washington County, way out in the country by the river, miles from any houses. I stopped the car and I put Sanka out, and I drove away. I left him all alone with just a six-pack of beer. When I looked in the rearview mirror, he was just sitting there, waiting for me to come back and get him.

"When Jimmy came home the next day, he went crazy trying to find him. I didn't tell him anything, except that we were getting a divorce. After that, whenever I thought about Jimmy, I had to think about what I did. I couldn't forgive him without telling him about Sanka, and I couldn't tell him. I couldn't tell anyone. When I saw him at the co-op, all healthy and happy, all I could think about was that he's changed so much, and I'm still the same person who killed Sanka."

She twists around to face Tom. His eyes are closed, and he's biting his lower lip; when she says "Tom," he lets all his breath out at once. Emily can't see tears, but she thinks he must be crying, and she hears in that unfamiliar sound the end of everything. She is getting up — unsure of where she will go, except away from that sound — when Tom clamps his hand over his mouth, and she realizes suddenly that he's laughing, so hard he can't speak. He sees her watching him and tries to talk, but he only laughs harder, a whooping sound that makes him grip his face until his hand stands out red against the white of his skin.

He sees her expression, and he struggles for breath. "Emily, that's awful," he says. "Oh, God, I'm sorry; that's the worst thing I've ever heard. I just keep seeing the dog trying to open the six-pack." He lies back in the chair for a second, helpless and spent, and then fights to sit up. "Oh, Jesus, I'm sorry. It just wasn't what I expected, that's all. Emily, can you forgive me? Em?"

He is waiting for an answer, but Emily looks past him. It is light enough to see the shape of things, and before she knows what's happening, she is laughing, too, at Tom, at herself, at all she did not know before about adaptation and survival at the beginning of the world, when everything was new.

Last Shift at the Mine

I HAD AN AUNT who lost her husband at Normandy Beach. She was standing at the backyard clothesline hanging up sheets to dry when she heard a car pull up in front and a door slam. In a moment she saw the Western Union man come around the side of the house, head bowed, holding a square of yellow paper. She didn't scream or cry — she wasn't raised that way — but she began to back away from him, holding a wet sheet tight to her throat. She dragged the sheet on the ground through a bed of newly planted marigolds.

I heard that story, my aunt stepping backward into a flower bed at the news that her husband had died at night and alone, over and over as a child. One summer at the lake my cousin Renée and I acted it out on the dock until my mother, watching from the kitchen, came out and made us stop. That night we did it again in my room in the dark. When we finally stopped, I lay on the bed with my arms crossing my chest and imagined scene after scene of myself reacting to a horrible tragedy. I would be sad, I decided, but mostly I would be brave. I was nine years old. My aunt died two years later, and by the time I was married I hadn't thought about her for a long time.

Everyone knew the layoffs at the mine were coming, but no one talked about them out loud. I was in my kitchen hanging the curtains my sister sent from Dallas for the new house. They were little white frilly things, and I remember I was thinking that the fabric might be too thin. I heard the front door open, and I called "Deb?" because I thought it was my girlfriend coming to help me with a dress I was making. She never knocks.

But then I heard the TV come on, and I knew it was my husband, Mark, home in the middle of the morning. I felt my stomach give, but I didn't turn around. I just went on hanging the curtains and worrying about whether they were too flimsy. I didn't know I was crying until Mark came in and put his hands on my face and they came away wet. He said my name, "Sandy," but nothing else, and after a while he went into the garage to work on the car. We went to bed early, but I got up at about three in the morning and came into the kitchen. I've never told anyone this. I got a pair of scissors and took the curtains down. I sat at the kitchen table and cut each curtain into long, narrow strips, and then I rolled each piece into what looked like a bandage. I learned how in Blue Birds. I put the pieces into a shoe box and put the box on the top shelf of the china cabinet, where Mark keeps the bank statements. I can't tell you why I did that. I just knew I didn't want anything about me that wasn't strong.

≈

I know a woman who still hears the 11:00 P.M. whistle that signaled last shift at the mine, even though it's been almost two years now since it's blown. It's different for me. When I think about the layoffs, it's the silence I hear. Mark and I got married just down the block, at Faith Lutheran; I was eighteen and he was twenty and already working at the mine. After the first layoff, in 1982, he stopped talking to me for almost two months. Oh, he'd say, "Good morning," and "See you later," but not much more than that. I didn't know what to do, so I just went on like nothing was wrong and waited for him to get over it. I was begining to think he never would when I found out I was pregnant. I drove back to the house from the clinic about ten miles an hour, thinking that if ever there was a bad time to start a family, this was it. I yelled at myself all the way down Simpson Ave. and I yelled at Mark down Grant and then I started crying because I wanted a baby so much. He came out to the driveway when I got home and I told him while I was still sitting in the car. I guess I thought one of us might be leaving. But he was happier than I'd ever seen him; it was as if being a father was going to fill the space where his job had been. He decided while we were still in the driveway that the baby was a girl and her name was Molly. I'd be sitting in the living room and he'd come in and carry on these long conversations with our daughter. And he'd tell me about her, like they'd already met and he knew all there was to know. About how she was afraid of cows but not of spiders, and how she flatly refused to eat anything but green beans. And he'd do her voice, too. "Hey, Mol," he'd say, "wanna have a steak for dinner? A steak and Mommy's lemon pie?"

And then in a high little voice, "Green beans! Green beans!"

I laughed so much sometimes I couldn't get my breath, and I wasn't scared anymore. We'd get by somehow; it was enough to be with Mark, this Mark who laughed and slept with his hand on my stomach. Seven months later, right after we brought Molly Elizabeth Coleman home from the hospital, Mark was called back to the mine. Molly started sleeping through the night at nine weeks, but when Mark was on the late shift, I usually got up once or twice just to check on her. This time I'm remembering, a light bulb in the kitchen burned out, and I went into the hall closet where Mark keeps his clothes to get another. There was a big box I'd never seen pushed to the back. It was from the grocery warehouse in Virginia, but I couldn't imagine what it was. I pulled it out into the living room — it was so heavy I could barely manage it — and lifted out the first of forty-eight economy-size cans of green beans. That was how I found out Mark knew another layoff was coming. I sat for a long time holding the can before I pushed the box back into the closet. I never told Mark I knew.

ᔕᕼᕼ

Sometimes when Mark has a temporary job to do early in the morning, like hauling wood, or shoveling snow for the city, and the baby's still asleep, I make breakfast just for myself and watch Phil Donahue on a Duluth station. It's what my Mom calls an indulgence, like eating a whole box of cookies back in the days when we had money to buy store cookies. I sit on the couch with a bowl of cereal and I watch people talking about stuff that's maybe a million light-years from my life. It's all this serious stuff — sex and politics and nuclear war — but I enjoy listening because I'm usually so tied up wondering what we're going to eat those last three days before I can go to the food shelf again, or where we're going to find the money to buy Mark new boots for the winter. So there they are on TV and there I am on the couch, and sometimes I just laugh. But other times I think about everything I have to do — and what I have to do it with — and oh, boy, I'd rather have a box of cookies than a sense of humor.

ᔕᕼᕼ

One day last week, Sandy got up early and fixed me breakfast, and then Joe Staley and I went to the central labor pool in Hibbing. We sat around all morning, waiting for our names to be called for day jobs like cleaning theaters and picking apples. When the woman behind the desk said, "Coleman, Mark Coleman," it sounded much too loud, and I bowed my head like I'd been caught doing something dirty in the back of a school bus. I wanted to just go on sitting there, but finally I stood up, and Joe and I got three days' work digging a well and putting up a fence for some people who bought a summer place on the lake. It was about 7:00 P.M. Friday when we finished, and we stopped at Swenson's for a drink, Joe because he was thirsty and me because I knew Sandy would be holding what she calls the "dinner show" for me, and that means tuna and noodles.

Joe and I graduated a year apart, but we worked the same job at the mine and we got our layoff notices the same day. He's never been a big talker, but for some reason, after a day of digging a hole, he started in about high school and how he wished someone had told him what it would be like to be looking for a job with a high school diploma, a varsity letter in track, and a layoff notice as your entire résumé. One thing about the last two years is that I've heard about a million jokes that aren't funny, and all of them seem to be on guys like us. It's true. Neither Joe or I are qualified to do anything but what we were doing when we lost our jobs. We drank about two beers thinking about that, and then we both started trying to remember what we actually did learn in high school. We decided that between us we'd gotten twenty-four years of schooling and a fifth-grade education. What does anybody learn in high school? I've been out four years now, and about all I remember really thinking about was how to get some sleep in Mr. Nyberg's third-period history class without getting caught, or whether my luck was ever going to change with one of the majorettes at an away game. I can tell you I slept more in class than I ever did on the game bus, but I can't tell you a single thing about American history except the three principal causes of the Civil War. And I only remember those because Connie Farmer helped me study for that test, and she was a girl who demanded a certain amount of concentration.

So I did my time in school, like I was waiting in a bus station, and when I graduated it was finally time to get on the bus — to go into the mines with my father and my brothers after summer was over. I remember that, all right, my first day on the job. My mother ironed my blue jeans and made me wear a new plaid shirt, and I felt like a kid following the big boys down the street. Except this time I was glad summer was over, because it meant I was grown up. I know that sounds silly, but I'd been waiting for that job a long time, listening to my brothers talk about what they did every day, wondering what the jokes about Sobrovich the foreman really meant, wishing my father would talk to me the way he talked to Danny about the mine. It felt so right; Jesus, I was even proud of how much I hurt those first few months, getting used to bending over and straightening up maybe a million times a day. So what I wonder now is, could I have made it turn out different? If I'd paid attention, sat up straight, joined the Math Club, retaken the SATs, would I have a college degree and a job that didn't come and go a lot faster than the tuna casserole waiting at home?

Sometimes — okay, times when I've had two beers with Joe Staley — I think, yeah, if I just hadn't been so stupid, it would all be different. There was a whole world out there, and all I could think about was doing what everyone I knew was already doing. I put more imagination now into thinking up stories to tell Molly before she goes to sleep at night than I ever did into choosing my "lifetime" career. That's the one that lasted two years. But then I think, Jesus, what guy would have been worried that it wouldn't last when it had just begun?

It's so hard to separate it out, to tell what's happening between Mark and me because he isn't working and what's just normal give-and-take between two people in a marriage. Lately I keep remembering this cartoon I saw once, where there were two little balloons over this woman's head. One read, "What I said," and the other, "What he heard." I feel like that woman; everything I say these days seems to mean something else.

Like last Sunday after church, when Mark and I took Molly up to the point for what she calls a "bicnic." She does that all the time now, switching *b*'s for *p*'s. For a while I tried to get her to say it right, but I've given up for now, especially since Mark's started calling it a bicnic, too. I tell him he's just encouraging her, but he says he's not going to worry about it until she's a freshman at Benn State majoring in piology. We were unpacking the sandwiches, and Mark and Molly were arguing about whether to go play on the swings at the "bark" after we ate. I listened to them for a while and then I said to Mark, "Keep it up. I've always wanted two children." I meant it as a joke, since it's hard to tell sometimes who's my oldest, Mark or Molly. But it came out all wrong, like I was accusing him, reminding him we'll only ever have the one child because we can't afford another baby. He was holding Molly's hand when I said it, and he squeezed so hard she pulled away from him and started to cry. He put an arm out to her then and said her name, but she was just out of his reach.

There was a girl who moved to Silver Bay in eighth grade, Christy Kuch, and she used to tell us all about her dreams. We'd be dressing for volleyball or standing in line in the lunchroom and she'd be talking about dreaming she was married to Elton John or got caught without any clothes on in the middle of the stadium at halftime on Thanksgiving Day. Pretty soon everyone but me was competing to see who could have the weirdest dreams. I just said I couldn't remember mine, because I didn't want to talk about waking up once or twice a week convinced I was falling a long way down. That feeling scared me worse than anything, and for a while I went to sleep every night with my arms above my head so I could grab the bedposts if I had to. I hadn't thought about Christy Kuch in years — her family moved again that summer, to Des Moines, I think — but I remembered her this morning.

Mark's in Babbitt until the weekend because he and Joe Staley got jobs helping to reroof the high school. Molly was still asleep in her room, but I knew she'd be up in a minute so I should go get breakfast started. I got up and opened the door to our bedroom, but it wasn't our hall. I mean, it was me standing there, but nothing else was the same. This hall had a dark-blue carpet, and Molly's baby pictures were gone from the walls. I was scared for a minute — if I wasn't in our house anymore, where was Molly? — but then I realized this was a dream and she must still be asleep in her room. And then I started laughing because Mark and I have been arguing for weeks about whether I need to get away for a while, maybe take Molly to my sister's in Dallas, and rest before it's winter again. "Now *this*," I said to myself, "is a cheap vacation." I was saying it in the dream, but it was like I knew what it meant when I was awake. So it was really like being two people, Sandy in the dream and Sandy awake knowing it was a dream. And then I thought, Listen to this one, Christy, and I started to laugh again.

I decided that as long as I was wherever this was, I should at least see the house, so I went down the hall into the living room. I kept thinking that I'd recognize the furniture or something, that I must have made the house up in my imagination from a picture in a magazine. But nothing was familiar — everything was new, for one thing, nothing from a garage sale anywhere — until I walked into this big kitchen. Mark and Molly were at the table eating breakfast, and it was my table, the butcher's block I picked out in the catalog. I remember thinking Mark must have just showered and given Molly her bath because their hair was curling at the ends, the way it does when it's damp. They looked so much alike, Mark reading the sports pages and Molly turning the pages of her coloring book. I said, "Way to go, dream," because I don't usually get the chance to stand around thinking how beautiful they both are. Just then Mark looked up and said he'd put an egg on for me. I sat down on a stool pulled up to the counter and he tossed me part of the Sunday paper. I wanted to tell Mark about it being a dream — he always makes fun of me because he can whistle the theme from "The Twilight Zone" and I can't — but then he started talking about everything he had to do at the mine the next day to get ready for the two-week shutdown for maintenance. I knew then that I had to wake up. I didn't want to be dreaming about what it would be like for Mark to have a job again. I'm the one who's always telling both of us that we have to face what's happened and go from there. Mark calls it "Mrs. Coleman's spilled-milk speech," and he usually puts his fingers in his ears when I start it. So I couldn't be having this dream about a different house and a different life; it wasn't fair to Mark. I said, "I want to wake up," real loud, and Mark looked at me and said,

"So drink some coffee and say it a little louder, hon. The neighbors behind us might have missed it."

I yelled it again, and then again, louder. And then I did wake up, because Molly was standing by the bed, pulling at the spread and crying because she was scared. I started to reach for her, to pull her into bed with me, when I saw I was holding on to the headboard with both hands. I knew I had to let go and take Molly, but I couldn't for a long time. Holding on was the only way I knew to keep from falling.

Three nights ago I went with Bev Urquhardt to a food-shelf meeting at the church. Donations have been falling off for a couple of months, and Pastor Robertson thought we should talk about what we can do to keep it stocked through the winter. I felt a little funny about going, since we use the food shelf once or twice a month now, but when I got there I realized that most of the other women in the room do, too. We hadn't been talking very long when a woman in the choir who just started coming to church came in with a reporter from the Twin Cities, here for another story about unemployment on the Iron Range. I started to leave, but then I thought I couldn't blame her for writing nonsense if I didn't at least try to explain what things are really like. And I did try. I talked about how hard Mark has tried to find permanent work and the way we've scraped to stay because this is where we grew up and where we want Molly to grow up. And how there's nothing sacred about wanting to live on the range, but we do want to, and we'd like to be able to earn a living here the way other people do in other places. At least I said some of that, until I noticed that the words were going straight from my mouth into the reporter's brain and then were being transformed into a sort of cartoon, "Nancy & Sluggo on the Range," a touching portrait of lovable working-class people fighting for their way of life against impossible odds. Buke, as Molly would say. I mean it. I hate the way what's going on here is shoved into these neat little slots that people bring with them and unpack at the same time they hang up their blue suits and silk ties. So, depending on what slots the reporters from Minneapolis or National Public Radio or the Task Force of the Week bring with them, either my neighbors and I are so long-suffering we make Joan of Arc look like a whiner, or we're clinging to the past so stupidly we sound like Popeye and Olive Oyl discussing retraining the work force. This reporter was a little different, though; she'd brought along the "desperation" slots, too, and she wanted to know every last juicy detail about what it's like to be "newly poor."

Bev and the other ladies were nice about it; they told little stories about how sad it is to see friends move away to find work and what it feels like to have a snowmobile repossessed or a check bounce for the first time — and then to have to give up the checking account because all your cash can fit in a coffee can with room left over for half a pound of Folger's. The reporter was nodding her head, "Yes, yes," and favoring us with enough Arpége to float one of Molly's toy boats when I imagined myself leaning into the circle and saying, "Well, yes, Lorraine, my husband and I do have some stress in our marriage beause he hasn't worked more than a week at a time in over two years. And, yes, we do feel pretty desperate sometimes. But you know what, Lorraine? A lot of the time we just feel horny. Really, I don't know what it is about living on the edge of financial ruin, but we just want sex all the time. I mean honestly, Lorraine, I'll be sitting in the living room of our tremendously mort-gaged home and Mark will be on the couch watching TV, and I'll notice the skin between his tennis shoes and his blue jeans — Mark never wears socks, Lorraine — and I'll tell myself there are things you can do without a job or a dime in the bank." By the time I'd finished making that little speech in my head, the meeting was over, and Bev drove me home talking about how this story might be a good one. I didn't say anything. I was thinking about Mark's skin.

Mark and Molly disappear when I spread out all the cents-off coupons on the kitchen table, the ones my mother gives me to help save on groceries. Mark says he doesn't want to know in advance what we're eating for another week; he prefers the suspense. I pretend to be angry, but I know exactly how he feels. I think the kind way to say it would be that our diet, like our bank ac-count, lacks interest lately. The other day I had the television on to some women's show where the interviewer was asking this Mayo Clinic doctor about the three major causes of depression in twentieth-century America. Mark walked through at that moment, and without even slowing down, he said, "Tuna. Tuna. Tuna with noodles." I splurged and fixed liver and onions for dinner. He hates that even more.

I took Molly to Dr. Martin today for her booster shots. When I bent over in the examining room to lift her onto the table, I saw my face in the mirror over the sink. It was my mother's face, the way she looked when I was a little girl. Because I was holding Molly, I didn't do what I thought of first — I didn't scream — but I plopped her down on the examining table and myself in a chair as fast as I could. I calmed down okay; I mean, I do look like my mother and I am Molly's mother, so I suppose I'll have to accept the fact that the only person who stills see me the way I was at seventeen is me. Lately, the worse things get, the more I think about that year, when I was in the Homecoming Court in November and married Mark in May. Oh, I don't mean I don't love Mark and Molly; I can imagine life without them for about two minutes, tops, before I run out of things to think about that don't involve teaching Molly to spell her name or playing Monopoly in bed with Mark when she's asleep. We both cheat, but I'm much better at it. So it's not that I want a different life or anything. It's not that. But sometimes I remember all the things I didn't know. And then I think I'd give anything I've ever had to be that girl again.

☙

We've been okay. It's not great without money, but both Mark and I work when we can, and we've still got the house. There's food on the table every night, and Molly has warm clothes and a new toy every time I can pick one up at a garage sale. We've been making it. But I guess we haven't been, not really, because Mark's given up. It started when he heard he hadn't gotten the job at the canning factory that opened in Hibbing. He took the phone call next door — we don't have a phone anymore — and after he told me about it, he stopped talking to me. I left him alone for a while but then I started getting scared, and I begged him to tell me what he was thinking. He'd just look at me, and then he started staying away from Molly. He wasn't mean or anything; he'd just put her down if she climbed into his lap, and he'd always have something else to do when it was time to read her a story. She didn't know what was happening — she's been his little girl and his Molly-face and his best buddy since before she was even born — but she didn't cry about it. She just stopped talking, too, and she wouldn't let me hold her for very long before she'd go into her room and close the door.

One night when she did that, I screamed at Mark to look at what he was doing, but he still wouldn't talk to me. I thought it had gotten as bad as it possibly could, and then last night it got much worse. I opened the garage door to take the trash out that way because the back walk wasn't shoveled. When I did, I saw Mark standing by his workbench cleaning a rifle. Mark's hunted all his life, with his father and his brothers, but he stopped about the time Molly was born. His dad brings us meat pretty often, and that helps, but Mark has never been interested in going along. I didn't even know he still had a rifle; I thought we'd sold everything like that a long time ago.

Mark looked startled when he turned and saw me, but he kept on running a rag — a piece of one of Molly's old flannel sleepers — up and down the barrel. I don't think I knew a human heart really could skip a beat. I couldn't have stood there for more than a minute, but it seemed like I thought for a very long time about what to do and what to say. Somehow I knew telling Mark how much I loved him or screaming or crying or begging him not to hurt himself wouldn't make any difference. He knows I love him, and I know that isn't enough right now. So I didn't do or say any of those things. Instead, from somewhere, I found the only words I knew would matter to Mark in the garage with a rifle. I said very slowly, "Mark, whatever you do, Molly will grow up and do it, too." And then I went into the house and got into bed with Molly and told her the story of how her father and I danced every dance at Homecoming the year I was a senior. I told her everything, all about my dress and the band and that ridiculous wrist corsage — only Mark would have thought of buying me a gladiola. I stayed there holding Molly after she fell asleep, and then I told the story to myself all over again. I didn't move when I heard the door into the kitchen slam and Mark go into our bedroom. This morning he woke Molly up with what he called a "get-up-time" story. He didn't say anything to me until tonight, when he said he'd sold the rifle to Joe Staley's brother. He said it wasn't safe to have it around with Molly getting into everything.

Sandy had a doctor's appointment this morning, so I took Molly to the library to see some kiddie cartoons. I wasn't paying much attention, and all she wanted to do was see how many different ways there are to sit in a chair. (Nineteen, if you count the handstand.) But I looked up at one point and there was a little character swallowing some dynamite. He gulped it down and then just stood there with his face getting redder and redder until finally he exploded. Except he didn't really explode; the blast was only inside him, so he felt it but he was still walking around when it was all over. The way things are going, I guess it shouldn't surprise me that when I do get someone to understand how I feel, it's a little guy with a red face in a cartoon. It's like I've swallowed everything that's happened to me since the day I was first laid off, and I can get the words to describe it as far as my mouth but not any further, no matter how hard I try. And lately I haven't been trying too hard, because I keep thinking if I don't keep quiet, I really will explode. The bad part is that the words about how much I love Sandy and what I owe her for keeping us all together the past two years are stuck in there with the rest of it. I just can't do anything about it right now, but someday I will say the words out loud. For the rest of it, I'm not a drunk, but I know now what they mean when they talk about one day at time. That's exactly how much I can handle right now.

We've known for months we couldn't stay unless Mark could find permanent work. We'd talk about it some-times late at night, but then it would be another day and we'd be doing anything we could to stay. I could write a book about that — about all the things we never thought could happen to us. Like going on welfare this winter, when Mark couldn't find any work at all for six weeks. Or my going to work at the Traveler's Motel three days a week, cleaning rooms. Two and a half years ago, when Mark got laid off again, we would have fought about my working at any job, much less as a maid. But not anymore. I know he'd do it instead if he could. When I come home on those days, he and Molly make me sit at the table while they bring me dinner like it's a hotel. "Madame perhaps desires the macaroni?" Mark will say, and Molly, who's started to swallow the beginnings of words, will punch me on the arm with her little fist and say, "Caroni, Dame?" I am never sorry about anything when they're carrying on like that. And as long as Mark is talking, I know we're all right. So we've been doing whatever we've had to — until two weeks ago. That was when Mr. Petersen told me there's not enough business at the motel and they don't need me anymore. We've been using that money, and whatever we can earn doing odd jobs, to eat, and drawing out what little savings we have left to pay the utilities. My parents made the June house payment. We let them because it looked like there might be a buyer if we could just hang on. There are some older people up here looking for retirement homes. But nothing's happened, and we can't wait anymore.

So we're leaving August 1; we've worked out a deal with the bank that will let us keep the house for at least two more months, paying what we can on the mortgage. The Staleys — they lost their house earlier this summer — are going to stay in ours and show it when they can. Mark has an uncle in Minneapolis who will let us live with him until we find jobs. I'm not thinking about what it will be like. I can't. I just have to get things ready here and keep Mark and Molly as happy as I can. I think Mark's glad. Even though he loves it here, I think it's a relief to finally have to go. It's like since we've tried everything, he won't feel any shame when the day comes.

I was in the hall outside the living room a minute ago and heard Mark telling Molly about Minneapolis. I had stopped to listen when I noticed that the wallpaper in the hall is pulling away from the wall. We bought that paper about a month after we got married, and I have hated it since the day we put it up. I started into the living room to tell Mark we'd have to start watching the garage sales for somebody's leftover wallpaper — and if he even so much as *looks* at a pattern with bamboo shoots in it again, I'll kill him — when I realized it didn't matter anymore.

I've been trying not to be sad about leaving, or at least not to show Mark how I feel. But it's been hard this morning, walking around the house and knowing it's the last time I'll ever stand at the kitchen sink or make a pencil mark on Molly's door to show her how much she's grown. Deb next door kept Molly most of the morning while Mark and I were loading the car. We had two garage sales last week to get some money together for our first few weeks in Minneapolis, so we're really only taking our clothes, some kitchen stuff, and Molly's furniture and toys. We sold the china cabinet, but the papers and things that had been in it were still on the living-room floor after everything else was in the car. I was going through them and throwing stuff away when Molly came rushing through the front door with her Mickey Mouse suitcase to tell me Daddy was leaving without me if I didn't hurry. I went out to tell Mark I needed ten more minutes, and when I got back Molly had found the shoe box full of white gauze strips rolled like bandages. I had forgotten they were there. I tried to throw them away, but Molly started to play, tossing them in the air and laughing. When she ran to the car, the breeze picked them up and waved them like tiny flags.

Rescue the Perishing

THE LAST SATURDAY of Spring Revival Week at my father's church, 1964, and at 4:00 P.M., when I should have been setting my hair to get a perfect flip like Patty Bailey's, I wasn't at home. I had dirty hair, unflipped, and I was sitting, uninvited, on the sofa in Mr. Becker's house at the end of Fitzgerald Street, waiting for him to come out of the shower so I could ask him to accept Jesus Christ as his personal Lord and Savior.

I was thirteen, and in serious trouble.

Patty Bailey said Mr. Becker was a Nazi — a real Nazi, from Germany, from World War II — and the kids at church believed her.

Two nights before, as the junior choir was waiting to march into the sanctuary singing the revival anthem "Rescue the Perishing," Patty Bailey had said right in front of everyone that she didn't think I believed in Jesus. She said, "You say you're saved, Ellen Ann, but I don't think you are. Don't you think it's time you really took Jesus into your heart?"

Dr. Bledsoe, our music minister, had called the choir then, before I could say anything, and when we paired up to walk down the center aisle, Patty cut in front of my best friend, Missy Tucker, and was right beside me, singing, "Rescue the perishing. Care for the dying. Snatch them in pity from sin and the grave. Weep o'er the erring one. Lift up the fallen. Tell them of Jesus the mighty to save."

I'd told my father I was saved when I was eight, a whole year before the first of my friends did it. My father baptized me on his birthday and took me to the Whataburger for lunch after church. Just me, without my mother or my brother, David.

Patty Bailey was right. I didn't believe in Jesus.

The night before, as Dr. Bledsoe directed the junior choir in "Jesus Loves Even Me," Patty had whispered that if I didn't let her lead me down the aisle to my own father to be saved "for real," she'd walk to the pulpit alone on the last night of the revival to ask for prayers for my salvation.

I wasn't a good girl, but I wasn't a Nazi, either; I knew that if I walked into the Saturday-night service with Mr. Becker, there'd be so much rejoicing over his soul — and over my part in saving it — that Patty Bailey might as well whistle "How Great Thou Art" on roller skates and call it a night.

My parents said I didn't think things through, but I saw some problems with this plan. First, when it came to eternal life, I had only the printed instructions to go by; if, as I was saving his soul, Mr. Becker asked for help beyond John 3:16, I was dead. Second, if Mr. Becker was a Nazi, I might be dead anyway when he saw me on his sofa. And third, if he wasn't a Nazi — if he was just a man with an accent and no social skills — then he was useless to me, and that night in my father's church, Patty Bailey would tell the congregation that the junior president of the Young Women's Missionary Union wasn't even a Christian.

My parents didn't believe I understood about consequences.

I understood that whatever was going to happen when Mr. Becker came out of the bathroom was a consequence.

I didn't understand why he was singing, in correct order, without an accent, the big numbers from *South Pacific.*

I should have gone home. I was no one's idea of a Well-Behaved Christian Child, but I still could tell right from wrong. Being in a stranger's house uninvited was worse even than helping Missy cheat on the "Identify the Flags of All Nations" test in Training Union so she could win an illustrated Bible for her mother's birthday. But I didn't move. I stayed where I was, on the old-fashioned, claw-foot sofa, listening as Mr. Becker strained for the high notes in "I'm Gonna Wash That Man Right Outa My Hair."

No one on Fitzgerald Street, not even my father, who was welcome everywhere, had been invited inside Mr.

Becker's house since he'd moved there the year before —
Patty Bailey said from his hideout in Brazil. I didn't
expect to see a German uniform hanging on a closet door
or anything, but there were no signs that anyone lived
in the house at all — no pictures on the walls, or books,
or plants, not even a TV or radio.

It was the smallest house in the neighborhood, too,
and it took me a minute to figure out what had been
bothering me since I sat down: there was too much furniture, all of it oversize, so that the living room looked
like my Victorian dollhouse at home when Missy
brought over her Western Barbie table and chairs. The
sofa was only a few feet from the bathroom, and as I
tried to concentrate on watching the door for signs of
Mr. Becker, I couldn't help realizing that I'd just been
introduced to a Fact of Life that would have horrified
my mother: a blurring of Our Lord's natural order, the
absolute division between the Living Room and the
Bathroom.

I didn't have long to think about the larger implica-
tions, though, because the voice coming from Mr. Becker's bathroom was getting louder. But the water noise
was louder still, so I was only sure of about every third
word: "Gonna . . . that . . . out . . . hair!" It seemed
clear that Mr. Becker was putting on a Broadway show
in his shower. I should have been comforted, in a way —
I was thinking, Show tunes. Nazis. Wait a minute! —
but I wasn't. I was less concerned with who Mr. Becker
used to be than with the fact that any minute now he

was going to open the door, see me, and realize that his afternoon stint of what my mother called Personal Attention to Personal Hygiene had been, in fact, a matinee.

To stop myself from imagining that moment, I thought about how odd it was that I knew every song (it was "Some Enchanted Evening" then) that Mr. Becker was singing.

My father, the Rev. Evan Whitmore, was the best-known Baptist minister in Fort Worth under forty, and he had a reputation for musical daring. He'd hired Dr. Bledsoe, who was unmarried, a Yankee, and, according to the ladies of our church, More Interested in How Things Sound Than in Winning Souls for Jesus. But my father's commitment to innovation had nothing to do with "secular" music, secular music being defined as anything written in the last century that David and I might want to hear. David, who was three years older than me and everybody's favorite, had been fighting a rearguard action for the last year to be allowed to buy Beatles records with the money he earned mowing lawns. The only result was that my parents had discovered folksingers — and folk songs about Jesus — and retaliated by presenting my brother with a large number of recorded versions of "Michael, Row the Boat Ashore." A weaker personality would have given up, but David kept trying. The truth was, my father had a soft spot that my brother was convinced could be used as a wedge to rock and roll: Evan Whitmore was a fanatic about Broadway musicals.

I learned the words to every song from *Annie Get Your Gun* before I learned the second verse of "Jesus Loves Me." One of the things I believed my father still held against me was that when I was five and old enough to join my family in our once-a-year concert for the congregation on Christmas Eve, I got mixed up and was halfway through my big solo, "Anything Jesus Can Do, I Can Do Better," before my mother could get to me. Eight years later, the ladies in our church still told that story to new members; it started, "Reverend Whitmore has tried so hard," and ended, "You know, she's adopted."

I was the only one who seemed to think it was unfair that everyone laughed at me while my father went right on loving Broadway. But he did, and so I wasn't in any doubt about what Mr. Becker was singing, only about what was going to happen when he stopped.

Thinking about my father was worse than waiting for Mr. Becker to come out of the bathroom.

Not very long before, I wouldn't have cared that what Patty Bailey was going to do would hurt my father much more than me. I was the lost lamb, after all; my father was the failed shepherd.

The truth was that a year or two before, when I'd put myself to sleep making up lists of all the different ways I could hurt my father, I might have thought of it first.

I hadn't told anyone, not even David, but in the past few months I'd started loving my father again, the way I had when I was little. Back then, David and I took turns standing by my father at the sanctuary door on Sunday mornings while he said his good-byes to the congregation. Even when it was David's week, though, I never went more than a few steps away. I knew that if I stood close enough, one of the older ladies would take my hand, point right at me, and say, "Reverend Whitmore, would you just look at that precious child? She's the image of you."

The Sunday I turned nine, while my mother stayed upstairs to cry, my father told me what some of those women already knew. I wasn't the image of him; I wasn't even his daughter, not in the way that David was his son. For a long time after that, the only thing I was sure of was that I blamed my father — for lying, for telling me the truth, for making it impossible for me to separate the truth about myself from the lies. That was when I started trying to hurt him, because every time I did, I believed that the look on his face was the truth revealed: a flesh-and-blood daughter would be different, she wouldn't do the things I did, and he would love her in ways that he didn't — he couldn't — love me.

I thought then that I'd always feel that way about my father; I knew things between us could get worse, because most weeks they did, but I never imagined that they would get better. But a month or so before my thirteenth birthday, I started waking up in the morning knowing that somehow I'd come back again to loving him. I was sure that what I wanted most in the world was for him to love me back, not in the "Ellen is my daughter and I have to prove it" way that was familiar to us both by then, but in the old way, when he looked for me in any room he went into.

About then I started closing my eyes when my father said grace at the dinner table. While my mother and David prayed with him, I tried to see the moment when everything had changed, the moment when I forgave my father for not being exactly my father. What I saw was the four of us in a crowded hotel lobby in Chicago. I was three or so, dressed in my best red plaid, and we were waiting for a cab to take us to the airport to go home to Texas. David was six, the perfect little gentleman traveler, except that he'd come down with stomach flu and was turning greener by the minute. My mother, her hand on David's forehead, was close to tears, and my father was trying to see to her and David at the same time. No one was paying any attention to me, and I climbed down from my seat and walked around the lobby until I found a man with a business suit and a nice face, reading a newspaper. "Sit," I said to him, holding my hands above my head, and startled, he lifted me into his lap. A few minutes later, when my parents noticed that I was missing, my father began a circle of the lobby looking for me, calling my name.

All of that really happened; I knew that because it

was one of my mother's favorite stories, and I saw it exactly as she described it: my dress, David doubled over, her own face pale with fear. But I added a detail to the scene, something no one ever told me. In my imagination, when my father came to get me, when he stooped to lift me from the arms of the stranger, I saw on his face the knowledge that he had searched for me, and found me, all over again.

I knew more about consequences than my parents thought I did.

I knew that I wished I could close my eyes and wake up loving Jesus, believing in Him, trusting in Him.

I wished my father could know how hard I'd tried.

☙❧

Everyone — even David, who loved me best — was going to get it wrong. They were going to think that my not believing in Jesus had something to do with my being adopted.

The truth was that I'd never believed in God. Not after my ninth birthday, but not before it, either.

When I was little, I was sure it was just a matter of trying harder, like with swimming. It took me four years of lessons, and two or three near drownings, to learn, and I still swallowed water and sank if I thought about what I was doing.

By the time I was eight, I was tired of waiting for a miracle to change me into a believer, and I decided to do something about it. What I did was say I was saved, right in front of everyone, because I thought that would give me a running start, like Missy insisting she was a ballerina when all she'd ever done was fall asleep halfway through *The Red Shoes*. The only thing was, Missy took lessons, and a year later she danced in *The Nutcracker* at the Civic Center. I said I was saved, and all that happened to me was that I wasn't just a nonbeliever anymore; I was a nonbeliever and a liar.

I never told anyone, but I knew something was wrong with me even before my father asked me into his study that Sunday to tell me I was someone else's child. And all the time he was telling me about the adoption, looking at the floor and out the window and up at the ceiling, looking everywhere but at me, I was thinking that it made perfect, terrible sense.

∽✇∾

The water stopped, and, a beat later, the singing.

I stood up like in church, the bathroom door opened, and I saw why *South Pacific* had sounded so American: the man stepping into the tiny hallway wasn't Mr. Becker. I squinted, trying to bring an elderly German into focus, but I still saw a man a little younger than my father, with brown hair slick with water and a navy bathrobe tied at the waist over a pair of khakis. Before I could stop myself, I said a silent prayer of thanks for the khakis.

The man hadn't moved. He didn't know I was there, but I couldn't get my breath, and when I tried, I made a squeaking sound high in my throat. He raised his head. My mother was absolutely right, I didn't think things through, and the man was looking right at me. His expression would have been funny if only we'd been in a Road Runner cartoon.

"Jesus Christ, you scared me. Who are you? What are you doing here? How did you get in?"

I was alone with a grown, half-dressed man who took the name of our Lord in vain. My secret fear, which always had been that I'd never have even one of the Life Experiences hinted at in my *Health Today* textbook, vanished.

The man took a step toward me, and I took a step back, into the sofa, and sat down hard. The impact must have jarred loose something important because I started to talk, so fast I sounded like Cissy Worley reciting, at breakneck speed, every single *begat* in the Old Testament.

"I'm Ellen Whitmore; I live down the street. My father's the minister at First Baptist, and I was waiting to see Mr. Becker. Do you know when he'll be back?"

"You know my father? You know him well enough to come in his house without knocking?"

"I did knock, but no one answered, and I decided to come in and wait. The carport door isn't locked. I didn't mean to do anything wrong; I just wanted to talk to Mr. Becker." He didn't look convinced, and I tried to imitate my mother welcoming a difficult family to church. "You're Mr. Becker's son? It's nice you could come see him. I didn't know he had children."

"But you know other things about him?" This time

there was no mistaking the disbelief in his voice. "You come by after school, and he gives you milk and cookies and tells you stories about his boyhood in the Old Country?"

"I don't know him that well. I just wanted to talk to him. Will he be back soon?"

Mr. Becker's son snorted, through his nose, and ducked his head, embarrassed. "Wouldn't that be something? If he walked in here and you popped up out of nowhere to say hello?"

He was still shaking his head when he walked to the sofa and sat down. I concentrated on making myself as small as I could on my end, a measly cushion and a half away. My stomach hurt.

"I should go home," I said, standing up. "I'm sorry I didn't wait for you to answer the door. I won't ever do it again."

He put a hand out, almost but not quite touching my arm. "Tell me why you did it this time."

"I just needed to talk to Mr. Becker. I really am sorry."

I'd started for the front door when I heard his voice behind me. "Here's what I think. You don't know my father at all, so you didn't come here to talk to him; you came in because you thought no one was home. You're a thief."

Being accused of something I hadn't even thought of doing was new for me, and I forgot about imitating my mother. "Oh, right, I'm part of a gang that steals sofas,"

I said, turning around. Mr. Becker's son closed his mouth, fast, and I could tell he was trying not to laugh. "I don't steal," I said, and that was true; it was practically the only thing I didn't do, but he didn't know that. "I wanted to talk to your father to help him, that's all."

Then it happened. Years of Sunday school, sermons, prayer meetings and prayers at home, church camp, and memorizing a Bible verse a week kicked in, without warning, and suddenly I was the brave missionary Lottie Moon, alone in China except for millions of Chinese, facing death for the Christian cause. I heard myself say, "I came to save your father. Jesus told me to come, and I did."

On that last word I closed my mouth and bit down because I remembered reading somewhere that fillings attract lightning.

"Jesus sent you? Who are you, Joan of Arc?"

"I told you. I'm Ellen Whitmore, and I live down the street, and even if I shouldn't have come in, you don't have to be so mean."

"What, you get better treatment in the other houses you break into?"

Sarcasm from adults was new to me. I associated it with Failing to Set a Good Example for Our Young People, and I took a guess. "Are you from New York?"

"Are you the Welcome Wagon now? Yes, I'm from New York. I live in the West Seventies, and I'm an actor. I have pictures and a résumé if you'd like to see them."

I said politely, "I would," just as I realized he was

making fun of me. "I guess New Yorkers aren't very nice," I added, and he snorted again, louder this time.

"Maybe not, but an amazing number of us manage to stay out of other people's houses."

"I told you, I was just waiting to see your father. Anyway, I have to go; my parents worry if they don't know where I am."

"I bet they do. I don't want to keep you, I'm sure you have other stops to make, but first I want you to tell me the truth about something. You owe me that much for not calling your parents to tell them you and Jesus are making house calls. You said you came here to save my father. Save him from what?"

"From —" and that was as far as I got. My mother held the southwestern patent on saying something nice or not saying anything at all; until I learned to read, I was sure Euphemism was a book of the Old Testament. But all the substitutes I thought of for the word *Nazi* — *murderer, maniac,* or, in a pinch, *maniac-murderer* — were no better than the original. "Sin" would have been explanation enough for most people I knew, but I didn't think it would satisfy Mr. Becker's son. Then it came to me, and I said, slowly, with a sense of having chosen correctly, "From his past."

I'm not sure what I expected — appreciation, maybe, for the tactful way I'd put it — but what I got was Mr. Becker's son standing up and almost running toward me. I was trying to open the door when he caught me by the shoulders; he was holding me too tightly, and he didn't let go even when I tried to pull away.

"Tell me what you're doing here! What do you know about my father?"

"Let go. I was trying to be nice. Let go!"

I felt his fingers on my skin through my Faith Camp T-shirt; when I started to cry, he took his hands away, so suddenly that I fell backward into the screen door. Mr. Becker's son was breathing hard; I was on the floor, but it came to me that he was the one who was hurt. The worst thing I'd ever heard about my father was that he was too high-church to be a Baptist, which didn't even make sense.

Mr. Becker's son turned his back on me and went to sit on the sofa again, as though I weren't even there. I got up, turning first to the front door and then back to him.

"I shouldn't have come, Mr. Becker; I'm sorry. I won't bother you or your father anymore. I hope you have a nice visit."

I thought he wasn't going to talk to me again, but he did, raising his head to look not at me but at a point past me, through the front door, on Fitzgerald Street. "Please, I need to know. What are people saying about my father?"

The revival service was less than three hours away. I thought about my own father, and then I saw Mr. Becker's son watching me, waiting.

"Not everyone talks about him; it's mostly one girl, Patty Bailey, who thinks she knows it all. She talks about me, too."

"What does she say about my father?"

I put my right hand behind my back and found the door handle. "She says he was a Nazi in World War Two, and that he came here after the war — well, not right after, but from South America, like you hear they do. And she says that's why he won't let anyone in the house, and why he's so mean if anyone tries to talk to him."

Distinctly, as though projecting into the back row, Mr. Becker's son said a word I'd never heard anyone say or even spell. He walked over to an old-fashioned break-front with drawers underneath the shelves and opened the second drawer. He put his hand in and without looking down came up with a flat box the size of a record album.

He was holding the box with his thumbs at the corners; I thought he was going to show me what was inside when instead he turned and threw it right at me. I ducked, a second too late, and the corner of the box hit me high on the shoulder. I went down on the floor again, with my arms over my face, but I could still see Mr. Becker's son coming toward me. He was standing over me when he stooped to pick up the thin red folder that had fallen from the box. As his hand closed over it, I saw, upside down, a picture of a little girl. Mr. Becker's son pulled me to my feet. He didn't move away; when

164

he talked, I felt his breath on my face and smelled vanilla wafers.

"My father's not a Nazi; he's not even a German. He came here from Austria when he was younger than you are. He was an American citizen before I was born. You want to save my father from his past? Try saving him from himself."

Mr. Becker's son went back to the sofa. He held the closed folder in his left hand and ran his right hand against the grain in the leather, over and over. My father held his Bible that way sometimes, and I waited for Mr. Becker to say the rest of it, to accuse me of bearing false witness against my neighbor, to order me to leave his father's house and never come back. I waited, but he didn't say any of those things.

After a long time I walked over to the carport door and let myself out. I stood on the impossibly clean cement, taking in mouthfuls of air, seeing the street where Mr. Becker and I lived. My mother's chinaberry trees covered the front of our house, but I knew it was there. In a little while I'd be walking down the sanctuary's center aisle with the junior choir, wearing my scarlet robe, singing "Rescue the Perishing" again. We never sang the hymn's third verse — it only took two to get to the choir loft — but I knew it anyway: "Rescue the perishing. Duty demands it. Strength for thy labor the Lord will provide. Plead with them earnestly. Plead with them gently. He will forgive if they only believe."

I let myself back into Mr. Becker's house.

As the door opened, I saw Mr. Becker's son move to stand up, but not before he put the folder with the photograph in it under a sofa pillow.

"Father," he said, and then he saw me. He said my name for the first time then, "Ellen," as formally as he'd pronounced the bad word a few minutes before. "Whatever you think you're doing, this isn't a game anymore. My father'll be back soon, and he can't see you here. You have to go."

Outside in the air, I'd thought about what I was going to say. I had a picture of myself picking through all the sermons I'd ever heard my father preach, stringing bits of Christian truth together like Christmas lights until I had my own sermon to say, just for Mr. Becker and his father. But when I looked at him, what came out of my mouth was, "Who's the girl in the picture?"

"Go home, Ellen."

"Is she your sister? Did something happen to her? Please tell me."

"You know I tell you everything."

Making fun of me put some color back in Mr. Becker's face, but he hadn't answered me.

"She is your sister, isn't she? Did something happen when she was little?"

Three steps put me at the sofa again, and I stretched my arm toward the place where the photograph was hidden, keeping my eyes on Mr. Becker's son. He was closer, though; he pulled the folder from underneath the cushion and held it above his head, out of my reach.

"I don't have a sister."

"But your father has her picture; she's someone he knew."

He looked at the clock on the breakfront. "Will you go home if I tell you who she was? Will you promise to go home?"

"I promise."

"Her name was Mary Tully. She lived in Brooklyn, two or three blocks from my father's jewelry store. That's a school picture; she was ten and a half." He stopped, as though I was supposed to think that was the end of the story.

I said, "She died, didn't she?"

"Are you going home or not?"

"You didn't tell me what happened. She died, didn't she?"

"She died, all right? My father killed her."

Mr. Becker had a beautiful voice; I heard that first, and then I put the words together in my head, one at a time. I was crying when I finished, but not because I was afraid. I wanted to let Mr. Becker know I wasn't afraid, but instead I said, "He's your father," and cried harder. Every time I tried to talk, I said the same thing, "He's your father," until I wasn't sure anymore what I meant.

Mr. Becker's face kept changing, and a couple of times he looked like he wanted to pat me. He said my name again, and then he stood up and disappeared into the kitchen. When he came back, he had a glass of water and a dish towel. He handed them to me and watched while I drank some water. I couldn't blow my nose on a dish towel, so I just wiped my eyes with it once and then held it in my lap.

Mr. Becker sat down and opened the folder, flat, so I could see Mary Tully's picture.

"Do you still want to know what happened?"

"I made you tell me that she died. I won't cry anymore."

"My father was on his way to work, and she ran in front of his car. He hit her just as he slammed on the brakes."

I thought about never looking where I was going. In the picture, Mary Tully's hair was in her eyes, pretty brown hair, and she was smiling for the camera.

"My father always said that when he hit her, she flew over the car, all the way to the other side of Market Street. He told it the same way over and over, except sometimes when he was talking to my mother, he'd say, 'She flew like an angel, Esther.'

I saw Mary Tully flying, and I knew, without asking, that Mr. Becker's son saw her, too. "It wasn't your father's fault. You said she ran in front of the car."

"It wasn't his fault. She ran out into the street without looking. But she was a little girl, and she died."

"How old were you?"

"Eight. My father went to the funeral by himself; my mother stayed with me."

"What happened —" I said, and I stopped because I wasn't sure how to ask what I wanted to know.

168

"What happened to my father? Is that what you mean? What happened was that he never got over it. My mother tried to help, but nothing she did mattered very much. The next year, she and I went to Philadelphia to live."

"Did you go back to New York to see him?" I asked, because I knew what it was like to have everything change.

"At first I wasn't old enough to go by myself, and when I was, I was angry at my father. I tried not to think about him."

"But you're here; you visit him now."

"When I was in college, he sold the store in Brooklyn; he wrote my mother that people in the old neighborhood were talking about him, blaming him for Mary Tully's death, saying he did it on purpose. He said he was going to move somewhere and start over. My mother called me at Penn State, crying; she said it was twelve years since the accident and no one had blamed him then, so how could anyone be doing it after all that time?" He stopped again and closed the folder.

"What did you do?"

"I didn't do anything that time. He left New York, but about two years later he called me from Boston. That was the first time I helped him move."

"The first time?"

"This is number seven. He doesn't hurt anyone. He takes our old furniture to a house in some city he's never been to before, and he stays a year or two, and he's rude

169

to people because he's afraid of them. Then he starts to be sure that everyone knows what he did, and he waits a month or two and calls me to come help him move.

"He's going to try Oklahoma next; I haven't told him that it won't be any different there. I come when he calls me, if I can, because he's my father and she ran in front of the car.

"No one blamed him."

❧

Mr. Becker's son and I sat on the sofa together for a few more minutes. I drank all my water, and then I stood up to say good-bye. I put out my hand, the way my mother taught me ladies did, and he took it.

"I'll make sure everyone knows that Patty made up what she said about your father. I won't tell them anything else, though; I promise."

"I know you won't."

"I hope your father feels better soon."

Mr. Becker's son seemed surprised that I was leaving, but I didn't have time to explain. I walked out the front door, exactly as if I'd been invited inside to visit, and started for home. I was halfway down Fitzgerald Street when I saw Mr. Becker turning the corner in his old Ford. I didn't want him to see me in the street, and I stepped up on the sidewalk. The car went by slowly, and I saw boxes from the A&P piled in the backseat.

I knew a lot of Bible verses. To be truly saved, you had to let yourself be forgiven.

When I got home, I sat on our front porch for a

minute before I went in. I heard my parents calling to each other from opposite ends of the house, but in my mind I saw the Beckers, father and son, walking up the same steps where I was sitting. They wouldn't want to come at first, but my father would tell them it was important. My mother would bring iced tea and leave the study smelling of perfume, and as the three men talked about the business of redemption, I would listen and consider the endless possibilities of being a good girl, an angel not of destruction but of everlasting love.

Legacy

IN BED LATE, climbing in and out of dreams in which his camera is a magician's object, capable of visiting both light and safety upon those he loves, Jack wakes, finally, to the sound of his daughter in the hallway. He lies still, taking in first the high tones of Kerry searching the house for her new tennis shoes and then, from farther away, the answering laughter and advice of his wife, Pam. As he listens, it comes to him that the timbre of their voices reflects their unfamiliarity with all the dangers of this world; they are beautiful voices, unprepared for sorrow. He loves his wife and child, and on this Saturday morning in late summer he fears he will lose them — though not to drunk drivers, or snipers at the mall, or boulders pushed at cars from freeway overpasses, not to any of the thousand calamities he has imagined might claim them. He is afraid now of separation and divorce, events so terrible, so ordinary, he never used to think they could happen to him.

He has known otherwise since the April day when Kerry dragged home from a neighbor's swimming pool, complaining that she was tired. She sat down on the couch in the living room, and Jack — his imagination leaping ahead to some mysterious paralysis — began to ask her questions about how she was feeling: "Does your throat hurt? Do you have a stomachache? Are you dizzy?" Pam came in in the middle, watching but not saying a word as Kerry shook her head no to each question.

When Kerry went upstairs to lie down, Pam looked at her hands for a long moment before she said, "She's not sick, Jack; she's just worn out from swimming all day. But now she's scared, because she sees you behaving as though she'd come home with malaria. Can't you see what you're doing to her?"

It was their old argument. Pam said his unceasing visions of doom were ruining their happiness; he said half the time Pam refused to see what was right in front of her. They went on saying those things, and worse, until Pam went to stand by the piano, crying a little, and said she loved him, but she didn't want to live this way anymore.

"It just keeps getting worse; every time Kerry or I cough, you imagine us dead of pneumonia. I'm thinking about leaving you." She stopped, white-faced and startled. They were still staring at each other when Kerry called down from the top of the stairs. "My head hurts," she said, and when they got to her she was trembling, hot to the touch with fever.

After they called the doctor, Jack and Pam stayed up

with Kerry, feeding her baby aspirin and orange juice, wiping her face with a damp washcloth. Jack was as gentle with Pam as with Kerry, and by morning, when Kerry's fever broke, Pam seemed to have backed away from her threat. But Jack knew he couldn't risk leaving things as they were. He thought about it all that day and then found Pam in the garden to tell her he'd decided to see a therapist. She was kneeling in a flower bed, setting out bedding plants. When he made the promise, she pulled herself up and buried her face in his shoulder. He knew then that he'd brought them back from the precipice — that Pam, his orderly, analytical Pam, had been imagining the end of their marriage just as he had.

Thinking about it now, Jack understands that going into therapy has won him a kind of temporary reprieve. He doesn't believe it is anything but temporary. Even on the days when he comes home from Dr. Martin's office and follows Pam around the house telling her about his progress, her threat is still there. It fills the air between them every time he looks at her.

When he cannot hear Pam's and Kerry's voices, he gets out of bed, only stopping to wash his face before pulling on jeans and a T-shirt. When he gets to the kitchen, they are already at the table, and he concentrates on cheerful greetings, with kisses all around. Pam pours orange juice for him and comes back to the table, leaning over to hand him the glass. He drinks the orange juice slowly, tasting his wife's smile.

Pam sits back down and begins to tell a complicated

story about TCU's religion department, where she's an assistant professor. He listens carefully, nodding at every pause to encourage her.

"Picking up pizza waitresses in the Sea of Galilee is not fieldwork," Pam says, and he is about to ask a probing follow-up question — "A pizza waitress?" — when Kerry catches his attention. She's finished eating and has taken her new camera to sit on a stool facing out toward the backyard, where she can look for "wildlife" to shoot: blue jays, their neighbors' stalking cat, Mustang, an occasional raccoon up from Kurtz Creek.

Jack is a photographer, a good one, and he gave Kerry her first camera, Fisher-Price pink plastic, when she was just learning to walk. The simple Nikon she's cradling in her lap was his gift for her seventh birthday last month. Watching her with it delights him: her seriousness, the tiny frown on her face as she lifts it to her eye and methodically begins to go through the steps he's taught her, her absorption in whatever she sees through the lens. He almost never looks at Kerry without registering how much like Pam she is. He does it now, taking in the sober, little-girl beauty that recalls his wife in childhood photographs, but thinking, too, of Kerry's joy in knowing things, in facts that can be looked up and verified, written down and memorized. Only when she is holding a camera is Kerry clearly his child, putting the world in proper order with her eye.

He hurries to catch up with Pam's story. "So what did Scott do then?" he asks her, making himself attend to her answer, laughing on cue when she says, "He introduced himself as a pragmatist!" Jack doesn't know what's so funny about this, but he loves the sound of Pam's laugh and wishes he had been its cause, not one of her New Testament buddies from the seminary. In Jack's experience, New Testament men can afford humor because their wives have already left them, and he's deciding how to distract Pam from their charms when he notices Kerry again. She's hooking her feet through the stool's crossbars and leaning forward too far over the flagstone tile, not holding on to anything but her camera.

After a minute or two, Jack can't stand it: he inhales and lets the air go, trying for the calm he's learned to value in therapy, but still he sees a picture in his head of what could happen, sees Kerry losing her balance and pitching forward onto the tile as he takes the first step toward her. "Kerry, sit up straight or come back over to the table!" he says.

Both Pam and Kerry are staring at him — his voice is much too loud, too urgent — but before he can apologize, Pam gets up to clear the breakfast dishes.

"Kerry, honey," she says. "Come help me do this, and then we'll make a list of everything you'll need when school starts Monday, so we can go shopping."

"I'll do it," he says, picking up his plate and reaching for hers, but Pam shakes her head.

"Go on and get some work done," she says, pointing toward his studio at the back of the house. "Leave us to our big decisions."

"You want me to leave so you can talk my daughter into a gender-neutral lunchbox," he says, going for a line he knows will make Pam smile. When it does, he turns to Kerry, trying for a smile double play, a tiny victory, anything to re-create the picture of a happy family at breakfast. "Hold out for Malibu Barbie, kiddo. You have rights."

Pam groans, but Kerry ignores him, intent on focusing her camera on some prize in the backyard.

"That's enough pictures for now," Pam says. "Come over here."

Kerry takes her time turning to face them, and when she does, Jack's amazed to see that she's crying. Kerry never cries, and he says, "Baby?" but Pam is already walking toward her.

When the two of them get back to the table, Kerry slips the Nikon from around her neck and puts it down before she lays her head next to it, still crying. The order in which she does it — care for her equipment is something she learned from him — goes straight to Jack's heart.

Kerry raises her head again and looks at them. "I can't go to school," she says, and Jack almost laughs because she's all right.

"Oh, baby," he says. "You'll be fine. Everyone worries at first about starting a new grade."

"You don't know. I can't go," she says. "The other kids won't know who I am. I can't go."

"Plenty of kids will know you from Mrs. Carson's

class," Pam says. "And the kids who are new this year will like you, too. It'll be fine, sweetie. I promise."

Kerry had put her hands to her face at Pam's first word, and she keeps them there now, talking into her palms. "I can't go," she says again. "You don't know." She is looking at Jack, not at Pam, and he says, "Lizzie?"

He expects some recognition of her pet name, the one only he ever uses for Karen Elizabeth, but she says, "Don't call me that, Daddy," and then, "It's not safe." The words don't make sense to him. For the first time in his memory, Kerry sees some danger that he doesn't see, and all he can think to do is keep talking, telling her everything will be all right.

He stops when Pam comes to stand beside him with a damp washcloth and hands it to Kerry, who wipes her face, hard, as though she's washing away dirt. "You'll be all right," Pam says. "Let's go upstairs and you can lie down until you're feeling better. We won't talk anymore until you want to."

Kerry gets up slowly and lets her mother put her arm around her for the walk to the kitchen door. Jack stands up to go with them, but Pam stops him, shaking her head. "No," she says.

"I'll see you in a little while, baby," he says to Kerry, and he watches as she and Pam walk out of the kitchen and up the stairs. He closes his eyes for an instant, not wanting to see their progress away from him. As he does, a picture rises in his mind: Kerry in her red scarf, a pile of leaves by the driveway, Pam with a winter perm, wearing her jacket from Eddie Bauer. He takes it all in, seeing everything, even what is not there. He is not there. He is not in the picture at all.

∾

When Pam doesn't come back downstairs, Jack goes into his studio. He ignores the commercial equipment that allows his mind to wander while he's working and instead sets out trays and chemicals for the old process of developing prints. He exaggerates every step of the routine, taking care to watch himself do things he's done thousands of times before. He has a print in the developing tray when he hears Pam outside, and he calls to her, "Just a second. Don't go. I'll come out there," moving the paper back and forth until his wife is smiling up at him. He took the picture at Kerry's birthday party, and he looks at it intently, wanting to believe it is evidence of something. Pam is smiling into his camera, wearing a party hat and making a V for Victory with her fingers. He reaches to turn off the safelight in the studio and, in darkness, opens the door.

"Is Kerry all right?" he asks. "Pam, is she okay? Did she tell you what's wrong?"

She is walking away, and he follows her into the living room, where she sits in front of the fireplace and looks not at him but at the rows of photographs hung on either side of the mantel.

"She tired herself out, finally, and fell asleep," Pam says. "She just kept saying she can't go to school."

"What do you think's wrong?"

Pam will not look away from the photographs, the three of them together, Kerry in seven years of sizes and poses and moods. "I think she's afraid."

Pam's voice is quiet, even, and he struggles to match her tone. "I didn't make Kerry afraid."

Pam faces him then, turning her back on Kerry's pictures. "How many times a week do you look at Kerry or me and imagine us run down by a city bus, or trapped in a fire at Safeway, or, Jesus, I don't know, whatever you saw in the kitchen this morning? What was that, Jack? Kerry choked by her camera strap? Savaged by raccoons? It scares me when you do it, you know that, and now we know it scares Kerry, too."

"We don't know what's wrong. I've never scared Kerry in her life."

"She sees how you act; you don't have to try to scare her. She knows you're afraid she's going to get hurt every second of every day."

"She could get hurt. I only want to protect her; even Dr. Martin understands that."

"You can't protect her, and neither can I," and now Pam is crying, her face so close an approximation of Kerry's that it's all he can do not to go to her. He knows by the set of her back that he can't touch her now, but he goes on talking, trying to make her understand. He stops when she interrupts him, when she asks, "What did you do, Jack? Did you imagine some bad man stalking little girls on the playground and tell Kerry not to talk to strangers at school? Tell me what you did to scare her."

He hears the certainty in Pam's voice, and then the words. "I always loved it that you could look through your camera and see something beautiful, something no one else could see until you took the picture," she says. "But I won't live with the other pictures, Jack, the ones in your head. They don't keep anyone safe."

His first visit to Dr. Martin was on a Wednesday. He sat in the waiting room, fidgeting a little, watching mid-morning light break in diamond shapes on the black-and-white tile. He told himself that if it would make Pam happy, he'd spend fifty minutes a week trying to figure out ways to put a cork in his imagination — to stop seeing cancer wards every time Kerry ran a temperature, or nine-car pileups on the expressway when Pam was a half hour late coming home from her last class.

All the sessions seemed the same to him at first. He talked about Pam and Kerry, about how much he loved them; Dr. Martin talked about fear and childhood, about theories of displaced anxiety. He talked about photography — how clearly he could see through a camera lens — and Dr. Martin talked about Jack's seeing Pam and Kerry as they were, and leaving the fearful visions behind.

He listened to everything Dr. Martin said; he did "imaging" exercises at home; he kept a journal of his thoughts, writing in it late at night, when Pam and Kerry were asleep. And none of it meant anything until

one Wednesday in August, when he sat up straight, remembering out loud his first camera, a brand-new box
Kodak, not a kid's toy but a real camera.

He told Dr. Martin that the Kodak was the only gift
from his father that mattered the year he was eleven. He
described it, every brown and silver inch, and then he
went on talking until all at once he was telling both
stories, about the camera and about his mother.

The truth was that all he had to do that year was be
a little quiet at the supper table, move his mashed po-
tatoes around on his plate some instead of eating them,
and the next day when his father came home from the
printing plant he'd hand Jack another toy and tell him
to get washed, that dinner would be ready in half an
hour. He liked the attention at first, but after a while —
he had trouble remembering if it was after the croquet
set or the *Junior Baseball Encyclopedia* — he started
greeting his father at the door and taking his coat, keeping up a nonstop monologue about his day, how great it
had been, how much he'd learned in school, until even
to himself he sounded like a comic on Ed Sullivan, one
of the desperate guys you never saw twice. He ate everything on his plate, too, without being asked, even yellow
vegetables, anything to avoid worrying his father and
getting another present when they both knew that what
Jack really wanted was his mother back again, the way
she used to be.

His mother wasn't dead, although when new kids at
school assumed she was, he took his time straightening

them out. She wasn't even sick. She was just gone, to Calvary Bible College in Kansas City, Missouri, because she said the Lord wanted her to train to be a missionary in Argentina. Before that, apparently, God had wanted her to be a wife and mother in Fort Worth and hadn't even minded that they were the kind of family that skipped church sometimes if the weather was good. One of the things Jack didn't understand was what kind of a list God could be working from that He picked mothers with one year of high school Spanish to do His work in South America. He even asked his father about it one time, and his father said, "Alphabetical, son," real fast, as though that were the only answer possible. He didn't laugh to let Jack know it was a joke, either, so that when Terry Wilder almost broke Jack's arm playing sword-fight on the playground that year, he didn't cry, he just yelled, "Your turn's coming, Wilder," and immediately felt better.

His mother had called a family meeting to tell Jack and his father she was leaving, and afterward she served ice cream in the good china bowls, ignoring the silence from her husband and son, silence so charged that Jack kept his head down the whole time, afraid that if he lifted it he would see what he was thinking floating in a cartoon balloon. "Mom's crazy," the words would say, because he was only a kid and that was all he could come up with to explain why his mother was dishing out Rocky Road on a school night while she outlined God's plan for her life. But his father was a grown-up, maybe the only one left in the room, and Jack finally tilted his head a fraction to look at him, hoping maybe he had it figured out some other way. He wished he hadn't bothered; the look on his father's face established a whole new category of looks, one Jack hadn't known existed until that moment.

The thing with his mother was like a newsreel: one minute she was there, prettier than the other mothers but not different from them in any way that stood out, and the next she was getting on the Greyhound bus to St. Louis, where her aunt Lois would pick her up for the drive to Kansas City. One minute she was in the house when he came home from school, and the next minute she was one postcard a week, three lines, signed, "In Jesus' Name, Your Mother." He knew that a lot of things had happened in between, and after, but that was what he remembered, moving pictures, just that fast. The speed was one thing, and for a while Jack thought that the hardest part to get over — much harder than the divorce itself, when his father finally got it — had been the absolute swiftness with which his life had changed: boom, no mother; boom again, a room full of Tonka trucks. But it wasn't. The hardest part was what he did at night in his room, when he closed his eyes and replayed every scene he could remember from the eleven years he'd been alive: all of it, breakfasts, vacations to Mustang Island, Halloween costumes, checkups at the dentist. Some nights he made himself run through them all, really fast, and some nights he picked one particular scene — the last Parents' Evening at school when he'd had parents, say — and stretched it out, making certain that he remembered every detail — what his mom was wearing, what his dad said, what everybody had to eat at the Picadilly Cafeteria afterward — before he let himself go to sleep. It didn't matter what he did; no matter how painstakingly he re-created pictures from his past, he never saw what he needed to see. He never saw the moment that should have tipped him off that his mother was unhappy, or was falling in love with Jesus, or had been crazy all along. That was the worst thing. Not to see it coming.

His mother had been gone four months when Jack asked for the camera. His father brought it home with him the next night, and by breakfast Jack had taken a whole roll of film, twelve exposures, pictures of his dad, of the house, of his Irish setter, Beau. Before long he had an exact record of the way things were for him in 1964. He kept all the pictures, even the out-of-focus ones he took that first night, in file folders that his father brought home from the plant. Once or twice a week he would look at all the pictures, one by one, searching for clues to the next disaster, the one he knew was coming. When he couldn't see the future in pictures of his father mowing the lawn, or Beau chasing squirrels out back, he began to imagine what might happen next. And every time it didn't happen — every time his father wasn't dead of a heart attack at his desk but was only late because he'd stopped at 31 Flavors for ice cream — Jack went to bed happy, sure he'd kept everyone safe for another day.

∽∾

When Pam stops talking, Jack goes upstairs to check on his daughter. Kerry is still sleeping, lying on her side, face to the wall, so that he has to bend over her to see the thin cotton of her T-shirt lift with each shallow breath. When he does, he sees her Nikon, too, half covered by the top sheet. She's looped its strap over the bedpost and crooked her arm so that the camera is inside it, safe from harm. He takes a long time straightening his back, and when he does, he stays where he is by her bed, not imagining anything but simply seeing Kerry, memorizing details and textures and context.

He leaves her room reluctantly and only because he needs to see Pam in the same way. She's moved back to the chair by the fireplace, and he starts talking before he gets to her, telling her he's sorry, that he will work harder with Dr. Martin, do anything required to put things right, give up any pictures not taken by his cameras, discipline himself to see the world without seeing only its dangers. He is talking much too fast, and Pam is staring at him, not making a move to stop him but not jumping in to forgive him, either. He's running down, knowing that in a minute or two Pam will tell him what she's going to do, when Kerry comes into the room. Her face is pink from crying and washing, and she comes toward them slowly, as though each step requires a separate and difficult decision. "Kerry," he and Pam say together, but she shakes her head, talking to her mother.

"Are you mad I found out?"

"Kerry, listen to me," Pam says. "No one's mad at you, but you have to believe me when I say we don't know what you're talking about. Found out what?"

Kerry looks at her mother without expression. "You promise it's okay that I know?"

Pam nods, giving up. In the next moment Kerry runs out of the room, headed for the stairs. He and Pam go after her; he sees Kerry run into her room at the end of the upstairs hall, but when he opens the door, she isn't there.

"Kerry," he yells. She appears, walking toward him from the closet, holding something wrapped in her Strawberry Shortcake beach towel.

Still without speaking, she hands the bundle to Jack, and he takes it and sits down on the bed. When he pulls the towel free, he is holding a Bluebell Dairy carton, waxy white with blue and silver lettering, exactly as he remembers it from his own childhood. Turning it over in his hands, he sees one change: when he drank this milk, the cartons didn't carry pictures of missing children. He looks at the photograph — a tiny square with a blurred circle in the middle, a baby girl's face — and feels the tightness such images always call up in him.

Pam has taken the carton from his hands and is reading aloud the words beneath the picture: " 'Karen Elizabeth ("Lizzie") Warren. Date of Birth: April 2, 1980, in Houston, Texas. Reported Missing: April 17, 1982, in Houston, Texas.'

"Oh, baby, she has your names," Pam says. "Is that what's been scaring you? That someone might take you, too? Kerry, it's horrible when a little girl's missing, but parents can do a lot to keep their children safe. You don't have to be afraid to go to school; nothing's going to happen to you."

Pam leans forward on the bed, reaching out to take Kerry's hands. Kerry allows herself to be pulled closer, but then she pushes Pam away and grabs the milk carton, running to the rocker by the window.

Pam says, "Kerry! What are you doing?" but Jack takes her arm; "Shhhh," he says, watching Kerry. She's rocking back and forth, cradling the milk carton in her arms like a baby doll — and this time he's sure. He has no time for imagining; he *knows*.

"Kerry, do you think that baby is you?" he asks. "Is that what you think we know, that you're not really our little girl?"

Kerry never looks up from the milk carton; she lets go of the words in a rush, the way she recites lessons learned by heart. "Her name is like mine, and she looks like me when I was a baby."

Jack hears the power the words have for her, hears how much she wants not to believe them but does, and he says, "Baby, can you listen to me? You saw the other little girl's picture, and you imagined she was you. But it's not real, Kerry; it's make-believe. You've seen pictures of yourself with Mom and me the day you were born, remember? You've always been our little girl."

Kerry watches him; he sees her struggling to believe what she knows to be true. "How long have you been worried about this?" he asks.

"Last week, you know, when I slept over at Amanda's. The milk was on the table when we had breakfast. I saw the picture, and then Amanda's mom threw the carton away because it was empty. I kept thinking about it, how she looked like me, and then I thought maybe you and Mom couldn't have a little girl of your own, so you took me. I didn't really believe it, but then I did."

Kerry stops and pulls the milk carton to her again, and Jack wonders when she will realize the rest of it — that the little girl in the picture is still missing. He walks over to her and takes the carton. The picture is of poor quality, grainy and dim, but he can see a faint look of Kerry at that age, a pretty little girl with dark hair and eyes, a big smile for the picture-taker.

"Oh, Kerry," he says.

"I didn't know what to do because if it was true I wasn't supposed to know. But then I started thinking the kids in my new class might see the milk carton, too, and they might recognize me. So I had to tell you I couldn't go to school. I don't want to be somebody else."

She looks at him, not her mother, trusting he will understand. "Oh, baby, come here," he says, and he lifts her into his arms, carrying her across the room to Pam with her hands around his neck.

"You're our little girl, Kerry," Pam says, kissing her, and he understands that the words are a kind of benediction.

∽❧

The three of them spend the rest of the afternoon together, Kerry modeling school clothes for her mother, Jack watching them both, trying to make them laugh. He can't talk to Pam because Kerry is always there, but once Pam says, "We'll talk later," in a way that lets him believe his daughter isn't the only one who's regained a measure of something lost. He knows just talking won't be enough to convince Pam to stay, but he doesn't dwell on the possibility of losing her. He concentrates on looking at his wife and child, making sure he sees only them, as they are at that moment, and nothing more.

Pam is calling out for pizza, with Kerry at her side arguing about the right notebooks for second grade, when Jack goes down the hall to his studio. Inside, he shuts the door and leans against it, closing his eyes for the last image he will allow himself to see. It's Monday, the first day of school, and Kerry has said good-bye to both Pam and him on the sidewalk in front, because only babies have their parents go with them to the door. He watches Kerry walk away from them, and he is raising his camera to take her picture, about to call to her to turn around, when he sees for the first time that she is not alone. She carries with her all the things he and Pam have given her. From her mother she has inherited her fine red hair; the vintage Dale Evans lunchbox; the curve of her mouth; and all her expectations of success and happiness. And from him, he sees now, his child has taken the Nikon on a strap, her good eyes, and her awareness of danger waiting just around the corner, waiting even in the brightest of new mornings and the happiest of times.

Things Not Seen

SEVERAL TIMES, when David comes home from the hospital to eat with his family, or calls Jenny to come quick and listen to Zanny pick out words in her bedtime book, or looks up at the bathroom mirror and sees Jenny behind him in the bedroom pulling on jeans and a sweater, he sees a difference in his wife's face, some subtle but fundamental alteration, and he knows she is remembering what has been done to her. At first, each time it happens, he goes to her. He stops the night she tells him to please wait, that she will come to him.

They have been married twelve years, David and Jenny, Dr. and Mrs. Harper, long enough to have an address book filled with names of friends crossed out as couples by divorce or some other tragedy, reentered as singles, then as halves of other couples, even as singles again. So disaster can happen — David knows this, feels it every day driving to the hospital, every year when he and Jenny open the book to address Christmas cards — but he has not really believed in it as a possibility for their marriage. They love each other; they love their daughter, Zanny (for Alexandra); David has allowed these strengths and the passage of years to make him feel safe. He has, in fact, awakened many mornings to a vision of their life together as fixed and nearly perfect; at those moments, he feels his love for his wife and child, all of it, in a single point just below his breastbone.

Remembering that vision — remembering what he sees now as his incredible innocence about the thousand variations of disaster possible, even probable, in this world — he thinks about what he has learned to be true: love doesn't make people safe, or keep them safe.

That knowledge, potent and terrible, was delivered to him whole on a winter morning just past when Jenny looked up from her easel in the breakfast room and told him about the recurring thoughts, the dreams, the unbidden images, that have made her believe she is remembering sexual abuse from long ago. One moment out of all the moments in twelve years, but it has cleaved time, and their lives together, into sharp-edged pieces of "before" and "after." They are living, the three of them, in "after."

Since Zanny learned to talk, she and David have played the same game every bedtime he is home from the hospital. There are no rules, just chasing and giggling and poking, followed by a triumphant "Touched you last!" Zanny is ruthless; some nights she gets into bed, pretending the game is over, yawns, and then, just as David starts to walk away, snakes her hand out from under the covers and finds his pants leg. "Touched you last, Daddy," she says, and then, just in case he is confused, "I win, Daddy. I win."

The second or third time Jenny goes to therapy and David stays home with Zanny, he stops the game when she starts it. After a time or two more, she does not ask for it again. He cannot think what he will tell her if she ever wants to know why the game is over, but he knows this much: he cannot pursue his daughter through their house to touch her, not even if she is laughing as she runs away from him.

David wakes in the light of wisdom, certain he has grasped some great truth in his sleep. When his eyes are open, though, the knowledge is gone, and its loss follows him to the hospital, where he is short-tempered and slow.

At midnight, eating the bag lunch Jenny has packed for him, he remembers his dream. It begins in the breakfast room, as Jenny tells him the fragments that have broken through the ice of memories frozen in childhood: a man in a blue sweater, a clean fingernail, a door opening and closing, the feeling of a weight pressing in from above. Everything the dream-Jenny does duplicates the morning when she did tell him, but in the dream, David is different. "Oh, sweetheart, there's always been something wrong," that David says. "I've always known. Anyone who loved you would have known."

⚭

Looking back, because there is no ease now in looking forward, David acknowledges that there has always been a caution in Jenny, a separateness. He has never seen it as a threat; when she has withdrawn in the past, he has put it down to her artistic temperament, waited awhile, and then gone after her, coaxing her back. He has always succeeded, and it has become part of their routine together — the dance of old married people, David calls it. But what Jenny is dealing with now is her own dance; he cannot find a way to partner her.

He tries. "Talk to me, Jenny," he says when she comes home from the sessions with the therapist. "Tell me what's happening, so I can help."

She tries. She sits on the edge of the bed, starts a sentence, stops, starts another, then shakes her head and is silent. "No," she says at last. "I can't. I'm sorry. I want to, but I just can't."

⚭

On an afternoon when Jenny is at therapy and Zanny is at school, David arranges for another resident to cover his patients and goes home. He parks in the alley, lets himself in the back door, and, without stopping, goes to the second-floor closet where Jenny keeps a box — high school yearbooks, grade school sketchpads, hundreds of pictures from every year of her life, college papers — that she brought with her to their marriage.

He lifts the box off the top shelf in the closet and carries it to their bedroom. There is too much Jenny in there, though, and he walks out of the room again with his arms wrapped tight about the box. He goes quickly into and out of every room upstairs. Zanny's is not possible; the room where Jenny paints is worse; when he tries their bedroom a second time, Jenny's presence is even stronger than before.

Finally he goes to the end of the hallway, where there is a window, and sits down with the box on the braided rug. The smell, old perfume and flowers, hits him as he pulls back the flaps — Jenny says her mother would put a sachet in the cockpit of *Air Force One* if she had the chance — and he smiles and sneezes at the same time.

He puts both hands into the box, reaching to the very bottom, and brings everything inside up with him. He places the pile on the rug and begins to go through it.

Everything that has to do with Jenny after childhood he lays aside. Halfway down he hits the layer that is grade school and earlier, and he slows down, looking at each piece carefully until he is satisfied he has really seen it.

He has not said the words aloud, but he knows he is searching for a picture of a man in a blue sweater. He also knows this makes no sense, and not just because most of the pictures are black and whites. But he does not stop. He goes on picking up pictures of his wife as a little girl, scanning the faces of uncles, cousins, visiting art teachers, coaches, 4-H leaders, for signs of guilt or exultation. He is not even sure which it would be, but he goes on with the task he's set himself.

He examines every picture, once, twice, three times, until all the faces blend together and he cannot tell uncles — men he has met and liked and shared beer and hospital stories with — from teachers long dead. When all the faces look alike, when all the faces look guilty, he understands suddenly that this must be what Jenny sees when she tries to remember. He thinks about closing his eyes and seeing dozens of faces, indistinct, culpable, fading away to blackness, and he says, "Oh, Jenny," out loud.

When he has seen all the pictures — when he has no suspects, or he has three dozen — he puts the pile in front of him back in the box, and the box in the closet. He holds back only one snapshot: Jenny, age seven or so, with her three older sisters one Christmas morning in Tyler. The four girls are dressed for church, standing in front of the tree, each with a favorite present. Jenny has a paint set in her left hand — he has heard stories about that paint set — but what holds him is her right hand. It is over her mouth, as though this were an ordinary gesture in family portraits.

Several times he starts to tell Jenny about the picture, but he stops himself, worried that she will see his search through the picture box as some new violation.

Jenny tries again to tell him how the therapy is going,

198

but the messages come out in code: "I'm all right," she says. "Don't worry about me."

David and Jenny both tell Zanny, together and separately, that Mommy and Daddy are working on a grown-up problem — nothing to do with her — and she needs to tell them if she is scared or sad.

Zanny waits two days and comes to their bed just before sunrise. She wakes them both up, first David, then Jenny, and makes a place for herself between them.

"You said I should tell you," she begins, and David and Jenny look at each other over Zanny's dark head, everything else forgotten.

"That's right, baby," Jenny says. "You tell us if anything's wrong."

"Well," Zanny starts over. "There is."

"What, baby?" David this time. "What's wrong?"

"I need twenty-four Valentine cookies today, and I forgot to tell you."

"Oh, Zanny," Jenny says, but she is laughing with relief, a breathless sound that makes her shoulders shake under the quilt. David laughs, too, and Zanny watches warily, not knowing exactly what is happening but sure that her five-year-old dignity has been compromised somehow.

When her lower lip begins its journey upward, David catches her in his arms as Jenny struggles to stop laughing. "We're sorry, Zan. It's just that you know how sometimes when someone tells a story they surprise you?" She nods; she has very definite ideas about stories.

"Well, that's just what happened. Your mommy and I were scared something was wrong, and then it turned out to be about cookies. We were surprised, so we laughed. You did right to tell us, though. We want you to talk to us when something's wrong."

She gives him the briefest of nods — apology accepted — before she says, "Well, what about the cookies?"

Jenny takes her then. "I think we're all awake now; we'll go downstairs and make twenty-four of the best cookies anybody ever saw." When David and Jenny go back to bed after the carpool pickup, they make love through a fine dust of white flour, white sugar, and silver sprinkles. When David kisses her Happy Valentine's Day and pulls back from her mouth, he takes a smear of red icing with him.

Many days they are kind to each other.

Some afternoons David leaves the house believing that what he says to Jenny, sometimes out loud, sometimes in his head, is true: everything will be all right. Jenny still has not come to talk to him about what she is remembering in therapy, but he thinks she will in time. Some nights at the hospital, he remembers the other David's certainty in the dream — "I always knew something was wrong" — with its disturbing implication that he should have seen disaster coming, should have acted, but he goes on to other things.

Other nights, when Jenny climbs out of dreams,

shaken, desperate for air, convinced that a stranger is in the room, David says her name over and over, until her face clears and he knows she is seeing him, not the man who is not there. "It's not your fault, David," she says then. "I know you didn't hurt me."

∽∾

Without telling David her plans, Jenny takes Zanny to a program that her therapist runs for children, on how to tell "good" touching from "bad."

David learns this in the hallway outside Zanny's bedroom, where he stops to tighten the laces on his running shoes and hears his five-year-old lecturing her dolls on parts of the body that are private. He feels the bile rise in his throat and goes into the bedroom, where he makes himself breathe through his mouth for a long ten minutes before he goes down to Jenny at the easel.

"What did you think you were doing?" he asks, pleased that the words come out evenly, as though he were asking about her mother's health or a point of art history. He takes it as a sign of duplicity that Jenny knows without asking exactly what he is talking about.

"I should have told you, I know that, but I was sure you'd think it was a bad idea, and I thought Zanny should learn what it means to be touched in a bad way. So I took her without telling you. She wasn't scared, she was interested, all the kids were, and she's handling it just fine."

The implication that everyone but him is handling things makes him so angry that he says what he is thinking without stopping to consider what will happen when he is done.

"How am I supposed to handle this when you won't tell me what's going on? God, Jenny, you've stopped talking to me, but Zanny has to hear all about what child molestation is? She's just a baby; we don't have to drag the whole world down on top of her because you think someone hurt you."

As soon as it is out, he regrets the word *think,* so much that he feels the nausea rising in him again.

Jenny speaks slowly, separating each word in a way that he has heard her do perhaps twice before but that he recognizes at once as rage. "I *was* hurt, David. And Zanny could be, too. Think about that and tell me again that I'm the one who did something wrong here."

He thinks about saying he is sorry; he thinks about telling the truth, that Zanny and Jenny being hurt is what he does think about now, day after day. But he imagines his daughter upstairs telling her bears what it means to be violated, and he makes himself be still. When he looks up, Jenny is gone.

He leaves the house through the back door and runs a mile, two, three, until he cannot distinguish the pain in his legs from the pounding in his head. He comes to a stop outside the park and rec center where Zanny learned to swim, and he sits back on his heels, taking in mouthfuls of air. He watches a group of children, still in their coats and school clothes, playing tag on the playground. A girl a little older than Zanny is being chased;

she is giggling, dodging the others, daring them to catch her. It seems to David, watching, that the boys who are playing are too old for this game, and too big. "Run," he hisses, "run," so loudly that a woman walking by jumps and hurries past.

David turns and, without looking back, begins the walk home. When he gets to the house, he finds Jenny and tells her she was right, Zanny does need to know about good and bad touching, and he was wrong. Jenny nods, the way Zanny does when some fact she is sure of is confirmed by an outside source, and she starts to walk away.

David touches her arm, lightly, using only his fingertips. "I'm sorry, Jenny. I didn't mean I don't believe you. I do; it's all I think about," he says, but she is shaking her head.

He looks at her, sees only exhaustion, and understands suddenly that this is Jenny, but not the Jenny he knows. At this moment, she is no one he recognizes; she is only a woman in pain, and he does what he knows how to do. He says, "We don't have to talk right now; you're tired. It's all right to be tired. You get some rest, that's the best thing for you right now."

"You're right," she says, "I am tired," and she smiles a little, as though he had made a diagnosis worth paying for. She turns toward the stairs again, and David watches her slow progress, trying not to think of what he will have lost if she is never his Jenny again.

Jenny dreams again, and sleeps late. David goes downstairs with Zanny to fix her breakfast. They are talking about school over bowls of cornflakes when David drains the last of his orange juice from the glass. "Zanny," he says, "if you'll go get the orange juice, I'll love you forever."

She gets up obediently but stops behind his chair to kiss his neck. "You'll love me forever anyway," she says, and he swings around and takes her into his arms, giving himself over to the sweet ache of her weight against his chest.

"You bet I will," he says, and he knows that what he is feeling is joy because this child has nothing to fear from him.

David stays late at the hospital. He remembers everything, discards nothing. He is a man locked — temporarily, permanently, he cannot know which — out of his wife's life, searching for clues.

As he learned to do in medical school, he writes down everything that will help in a diagnosis. He starts with what Jenny has told him about her childhood in east Texas. He knows her family, of course: her schoolteacher mother, Dorothy; her three older sisters and their husbands; the knot of maternal cousins and aunts and uncles that crowd the annual Scherer family reunions.

He goes on to the story of her banker father, who had a heart attack at his desk at First National two weeks after his thirty-sixth birthday and died before the ambulance could come for him. Jenny was born three months after the funeral, and David knows that her father — the Man Who Wasn't There — was the central legend of her childhood. He thinks about the house of women in which Jenny grew up; he remembers her stories about asking to sleep over with friends in elementary school just so she could watch their fathers come down to breakfast, dressed for work and smelling of Old Spice.

David turns over a page in his notebook to list the names of the men he can remember Jenny talking about from her childhood. When he is done, the list is short — only four names — and David stops because all he can see is Jenny as a little girl, and the picture is so like Zanny that the tightness in his chest is impossible to ignore.

He sits up straight and looks at the names, considering each in turn: Jenny's uncle Ed, who took the girls camping every summer at Big Bend; her best friend Sally's dad, who escorted both girls to the father-daughter dinners the church held every Valentine's Day; her older sister Donna's boyfriend Mark, who was always in the house until he went into the army, when Jenny was nine; and Bob Finley, the man her mother said was going to marry her and be the girls' new father.

Jenny was five when her mother met Mr. Finley — he managed Tyler's only hotel, and they met in a

night-school course he taught on starting a catering business — and six when her mother came home and said
she'd been wrong, that Mr. Finley wasn't the man for
them. The older girls cried, David remembers Jenny saying, but in time Mr. Finley became a family joke, short-
hand for a narrow escape, and the term is still used when
the sisters are together with their mother. Jenny doesn't
laugh, though; David sees that now, recalling the last
time the family was gathered for a reunion. Jenny never
laughs at Mr. Finley, and David puts the notebook on
the table. He picks it up after a second and holds it away
from him toward the light, the way he has been taught
to hold X rays confirming the presence of disease.

Jenny asks David to come with her to her next session
with the therapist. All that day David is nervous, elated,
expectant; the phrases that come into his head are clichés,
words his own father would use in tracking down the
source of a pinging sound in the Ford. Now we're getting somewhere, he thinks. Now we'll get to the bottom
of this. He reaches for the phone to tell Jenny he is turning into his father — it has been a serious fear of his,
and a favorite joke of hers, since Zanny was born — but
he stops. Talking about his father is just something else
he can't do with Jenny right now, and he feels his elation
slip away.

They drive to the clinic separately, Jenny from home,
David from the hospital. When David walks into the

building, the elevator doors are closing on a dark-haired woman in a camel's-hair coat, smoking a cigarette. The woman is Jenny, who has never smoked; David walks up the stairs slowly, uncertain of where he is going.

The session is fifty-five minutes long. The therapist, a motherly woman in a gray suit, talks about the process of healing; Jenny talks about her fears, and David talks about his.

There are moments when David and Jenny talk together, moments when they see each other clearly and know it, moments when they both smile.

As he walks out of the session with Jenny, his hand under her elbow, this is the moment David remembers: the therapist, explaining one "dynamic" of abused children, says, "Women who have been abused may grow up to marry abusers."

He remembers that moment because of the next. Jenny does not say, "But I didn't do that." Jenny does not say, "David's never hurt me." Jenny does not say, "What happened to me in the past has nothing to do with my marriage." She is silent, and even knowing the silence may mean a hundred different things, he has to grit his teeth against the word *betrayal*.

Now, walking with Jenny toward their cars, he knows that the words *innocence* and *guilt* have different meanings, but with the taste of *betrayal* in his mouth he cannot think what they might be.

As he opens the car door for Jenny, he says, "Now

we're getting somewhere," swallowing laughter as tears come to his eyes. Jenny looks at him, not understanding either; he remembers that, too.

∽◈◇

Jenny stops painting pictures of people, real or imagined. The canvases that come and go in the breakfast room are still lifes now: a medical book on a straight-backed chair; a child's coat slumped against the wall in a room with too many plants; a row of brightly painted doors, opening and closing.

∽◈◇

Jenny continues seeing the therapist; every fifth session or so, David goes with her. More and more Jenny talks about feeling trapped, feeling forced to satisfy everyone but herself. David listens; each word travels somewhere inside him. The certainty comes to him that if he is cut open someday, the surgeon holding the scalpel will have to turn those words over to reach his heart.

He thinks about lying, about saying, "I don't want anything from you, Jenny," but he tells the truth: "I want this to be over. I want you to be okay. I want things to be the way they were."

"What if they can't be?" Jenny says. "What if I'm okay and things still aren't the same? What if they never are?"

∽◈◇

At times Jenny longs for closeness, needs it, seeks it out; they make love now only during those times, only when Jenny begins it. He responds to her, moving closer if she pulls at him, moving away if she pushes. They are done when she is done, when she says his name and rolls away to the far edge of the bed. Sometimes, toward morning, she turns back to him and puts a hand to his face.

He is always at the hospital now; he has discovered his patients again, the way first-year medical students do after they finish an exam rotation. He is gentle when people are afraid; he is efficient when they are demanding; he is especially good with families that are waiting for the outcome of a test or procedure. He is not sure why that is until it comes to him as he is patting the hand of a woman whose husband is impotent: second-hand pain, he thinks.

He feels a pressure in his chest. It is there when he wakes up, when he reads to Zanny, when he talks to Jenny's mother on the phone. It builds or subsides depending on how he and Jenny are together; what it does not do is go away.

He wonders about Zanny — he knows she sees the difference in the house, in him and Jenny — but she responds to every question of his with one of her own.

"Are you okay, baby?"

"Are you okay, Daddy?"

"I'm fine, baby."

"I'm fine, too."

"Then everyone here is fine."

"Fine."

He is touched that his child is brave. He worries that she will grow up a liar.

❦

David sees menace everywhere: in the unshaven faces of parking-lot attendants, in the junior-high paperboy, in bank tellers, in the lingering smiles of TV anchormen.

At the local market, the old man bagging their groceries stoops to hand Zanny a red sucker, as he always does. David intercepts it and hands it back. "Thanks, but we're cutting down."

Zanny is quiet in the car, not sulking but thoughtful, and just before they get home, he turns back toward the shopping center. He and Zanny have french fries and hot chocolate at the Dairy Queen. They sit on the same side of the booth, Zanny nearest the wall. David talks to his daughter about kindergarten, leaning forward slightly so she is hidden from the sight of a middle-aged man in a telephone-company uniform, alone in the booth opposite.

❦

David sees Jenny trying: she surprises him with small presents — argyle socks that will seem ridiculous with his hospital blues, a new flashlight — and one day he opens his lunch at the hospital to find that his tuna sandwiches, like Zanny's, have been cut into heart shapes. She begins a painting of Zanny for his birthday. In his thank-yous he does not tell Jenny how affecting he finds all this, or how sad.

He is thinking about it when she comes into the kitchen and sits beside him. "I love you," she says. "I don't want to hurt you. I'm just so scared all the time. Remembering scares me. Not remembering scares me. When I feel that way, I can't talk. I have to protect myself, even from you."

Jenny has begun to cry, softly, the way Zanny does when she believes she has been wronged but sees no hope of justice. David rises, takes a step toward her chair, and bends to kiss her face. "I'm scared, too. I'm afraid I'll do something to make it worse. I'm afraid I'll lose you."

Looking at Jenny's face, he realizes that she has matched him in imagining disasters; she, too, has seen all the possibilities. Kissing her again, he says the only words he can think of that are both true and safe: "I love you, too. I'm sorry you were hurt; I never want anything to hurt you." He hears how weak his reassurances sound — what has he done, after all, to keep her safe? — but Jenny accepts them as comfort.

He feels his love for her and Zanny, all of it, in his chest, where the tightness builds, crests, eases but does not go away, even now.

In bed Jenny lies in David's arms until she falls asleep. He watches her, feeling that at least some of the crisis between them has passed, unwilling to consign her to darkness. When he finally sleeps, he starts in and out of dreams in which his sickest patients grow old, irritable, expert at bridge, but never die. Jenny and Zanny are there, too, eating ice cream, laughing, throwing their faces back to catch the sun. They are beautiful, his wife and child, and he is smiling at them when the dream ends. When it does, when he opens his eyes in the darkness, he knows that Jenny is gone.

He rises on a run, fighting down panic that doubles with every breath. In the hallway he stands for a minute, listening, and then begins to walk toward Zanny's door.

The door is open an inch or so, enough that David can see Jenny kneeling by Zanny's bed. The room is dark, lit only by the Wonder Woman lamp, so he cannot see their expressions, only that Jenny is kneeling and Zanny is half sitting up against her pillows.

He cannot quite make out their words — their voices are too soft — but he sees their closeness, hears them laugh, and understands that Jenny has left their bed to seek comfort in being with their daughter. He sees Zanny's hand dart out from the covers and knows she is saying, "Touched you last, Mommy; I win."

Seeing that, David opens the door; he wants nothing more at this moment than to be with them, to feel the three of them together against the darkness that is everywhere.

He has taken only one step into the room when he hears Jenny gasp, sees her reach to gather Zanny into her arms and turn so that the child is hidden from sight.

"Jenny, it's me," David says. "It's me." He does not

wait but moves toward them slowly, silently, fixing in his mind the image of his wife and daughter holding each other for comfort, huddled together against the figure of a man in a doorway, his face and intent unrecognizable in the darkness.